...MMERS

Never Bite a Boy on the First Date

HARPER TEEN

An Imprint of HarperCollinsPublishers

Library of Congress catalog card number:
2009920735
ISBN 978-0-06-172154-0

Typography by Andrea Vandergrift
09 10 11 12 13   OPM   10 9 8 7 6 5 4 3 2 1
❖
First Edition

𝓘 love Fridays just as much now that I'm a vampire as I did when I was human. I take full advantage of the weekends—mainly to sleep all day. At least, I do when I'm not in the middle of a murder investigation and, apparently (much to my surprise), dating three boys at once.

It started with Daniel, Friday morning. He was already at his desk when I got to history class, and from the moment I walked in the room I could feel him watching me. I mean, he didn't take his eyes off me as I came down the row to my desk, and I wasn't even wearing anything special—just jeans and a sunny yellow off-the-shoulder shirt and ankle boots. And sunflower earrings. And maybe a couple of tiny yellow butterfly clips in my hair. All right, I might have been feeling a little cheerful when I got dressed. Sure, I had been accused of murder by my family and was wrapped up in a bizarre investigation, but there were such *cute* boys involved.

Plus I thought Milo and Rowan would appreciate the look . . . and judging from the expression on his face, Daniel did, too.

Hey, I try to look on the bright side.

Also by
TAMARA SUMMERS

Save the Date

For Rachel A., because you're awesome, and because I bet you could solve a murder, juggle three boys, and fit through a cat flap, no problem. :-)

And for Kari, because obviously.

Never Bite
a Boy on the
First Date

Prologue

If you were dying . . .

If you were sixteen and dying . . .

If your blood was spilling out of you, calling to them, the creatures of the night, and you knew you were dying . . .

If you saw their pale faces and the gleam of sharp teeth in the moonlight, and you felt your blood spilling warmly over your hands, and you knew beyond any doubt that you were dying . . .

Wouldn't you say yes?

Yes, turn me.

Yes, I want to live.

Yes . . . make me one of you.

Chapter 1

There's a murderer in my school. And this time it isn't me, so I'm kind of ticked off.

The body was lying on the front steps of Luna High School, upside down. His blood was running all the way down the steps to the ground, like a red carpet laid out to welcome us inside. He was wearing a red-and-gold Luna Tigers football jersey and a startled expression. I guess being thrown out of a third-story window would surprise me, too. The broken window-panes creaked ominously up above, and shattered glass sparkled in the blood around him, reflecting the morning sunlight.

We could smell the blood the minute we pulled into the parking lot. I heard Zach's stomach growl, which, if you ask me, is a totally inappropriate reaction. And also ridiculous, since he'd had, like, two gallons of blood for breakfast already.

At the bottom of the steps, a couple of policemen were speaking into their walkie-talkies and trying to fend off all the curious teenagers who were early for school. Mostly that included the swim team and kids whose parents have to get to work early. Plus students like me and Zach, who prefer to be indoors before the sun is fully up.

Don't worry, we're not going to burst into flames or anything. That's a myth. Go back and read *Dracula*, and you'll see—the sun just drains his powers; it doesn't kill him. Not that I'm saying Bram Stoker was an expert or anything, but he's kind of right about that part.

So I don't die in a ball of fire the moment I step outside, which is a plus. But the bad news is that too much direct sunlight gives me a wicked headache, and then I have to lie in a dark room for a while to recover. It's kind of like having a mild sun allergy. It gets worse for older vampires, who have less tolerance. We also cover ourselves in this crazy herbal sunscreen, which helps a little bit, although I think it makes me smell like basil.

Basically it sucks, since I no longer have to worry about skin cancer, so I should be able to tan as much as I want. Instead, I'm stuck with the skin tone I had when I died. Not that we get a ton of sunshine in freezing Massachusetts anyway. Luckily for me, the pale look is coming back in. (It *is* coming back in, isn't it?)

Right. Back to the dead guy.

There was one more thing we could spot from across the parking lot. The police wouldn't know what they were looking at, but to vampires like us, the big holes in his neck were a dead giveaway. (Ha ha! Hilarious pun! I know, stake me now.)

Where does the image of two perfect little puncture wounds come from anyway? You see that everywhere, but it's kind of physically impossible to do, and I should know—I have actually tried this experiment. Yeah, you've got your fangs up top, but you also have two sharp little fangs on the bottom, and the only way to really latch on and get all the blood you need is to bite with all of them, which leaves *four* tiny little puncture wounds—and that's if you're neat.

More often, as in this case, it leaves a bloody mess.

I've got those four little scars on my neck and my wrist—one set from Olympia (my vampire "mom") and one from Crystal (my vampire "sister"). I hide the marks with my hair and my watch, and they kind of look like freckles now. Creepy freckles, but it could be worse.

I could be missing half my neck, like this guy.

"Gross," Zach offered from the backseat, leaning forward to peer over my shoulder. I edged closer to the window, away from him, but he didn't seem to notice. "Someone needs to work on her technique."

Olympia parked the car and turned to stare at me with her big, dark, *I know everything* eyes.

"I didn't do it," I said immediately.

"Kira—" she started.

"I *knew* you would think it was me! That's so unfair! I swear, I didn't do it! Oh, my God, make *one* mistake and suddenly every vampire attack is my fault."

"You must admit it's odd," Olympia said. "Two vampire attacks in two towns in a row.

6

Before you came along, I managed to go twenty-five years without seeing any vampire attacks in public like this."

"Okay, I agree it's weird, but this wasn't me," I said. "I *swear*."

It's true, you don't see a vampire attack every day. In fact, you hardly ever see one. All the rules about this were drummed into my head from the moment I woke up with fangs, and then re-drummed again after my little mistake last year.

"Besides, I'm not the eat-'em-and-leave-'em type, remember?" I added.

"Hey, that's Tex Harrison," Zach said, squinting through the windshield at the body.

"No way," I said. We'd only been here a month, but even I knew Luna's star quarterback. "How can you tell?"

"His football jersey," Zach said. "Number nine? Hello?"

As if I would know that.

"See!" I said, turning to Olympia. "That proves I didn't do it! I would never bite a Neanderthal like Tex Harrison. His blood probably tastes like beer and Cheetos."

7

Olympia rolled her eyes. She does that a lot. Possibly just around me. I think she's beginning to wonder if bringing a sixteen-year-old vampire into the gang was such a good idea. It's still unclear whether I'm going to act sixteen for the rest of my immortal life. If you ask me, I'd say I'm already *way* more mature than I was a year ago, so I don't think she has anything to worry about. *I'm* the one who has to worry, because it's probably not going to be fun to be twenty-nine in a sixteen-year-old body . . . or fifty . . . or five hundred. If I have to go to high school over and over again for the rest of eternity, I will seriously decapitate myself.

Olympia always says, "Let's cross that bridge when we come to it," meaning when I manage to actually get through an entire school year without some big, dramatic death (mine, for instance) forcing us to move. On the plus side, by the third time around, U.S. History is a total breeze . . . although, sadly, not any less boring.

"Is he going to wake up like us?" Zach asked. "I mean, will he be a vampire? Should we stake out his grave?"

Olympia winced at his choice of words. She's

a little sensitive about things that can kill us. Hardly anything in our house is made of wood, for instance.

"It depends," Olympia said. "If he was bitten before he died, then yes, he'll become a vampire." She pointed at the river of blood dripping down the steps. "But judging from that, he was killed first and then bitten. Otherwise the vampire would have drained much more from him before tossing him out the window. My guess is that the vampire decided to have a snack after throwing him through the glass, but she—"

"Or he!" I protested.

"—was probably interrupted, since there's still so much blood inside the corpse, too."

"This," I said, "is a seriously sick conversation." I haven't entirely adjusted to the whole *yum, blood, yum* aspect of being a vampire. My body wants it, but my head is still like, *Ew, that is BLOOD, time to faint.*

"I'll have to talk to Wilhelm about this," Olympia said with a sigh. Wilhelm is my vampire "dad." (He prefers the word "patriarch." If you call him Dad, even ironically, he will flail his pale arms around and make outraged huffing

9

noises through his moustache.) He mostly lies in his coffin, •brooding and issuing proclamations about how degenerate the world is today. Apparently things have gone way downhill since, like, the Middle Ages.

"Well, tell him I said I didn't do it," I said.

"Who else could it be?" Zach said. Very helpful. Thanks, Zach.

"It could be *you*," I suggested. "Whoever said *you* had good impulse control?"

That was kind of a low blow, I'll admit. He flushed angrily, which was only possible, by the way, because of that two-gallons-of-blood breakfast I mentioned earlier.

"*I* was on a blood run with Bert last night," he said icily.

"That's true," Olympia agreed. "They were gone for hours."

"Where were *you*?" Zach asked.

Out by myself, as usual, which he totally knew. If I'd known *he* was out, I might have stayed home and watched TV instead. But I'm in Zach-avoidance mode, which means lots of long, solitary midnight walks until I'm sure he's asleep. (He's still on a more human schedule than the rest of us.) Doesn't make for a great alibi, unfortunately.

"At the cemetery," I said with a sigh. I know—I'm such a cliché. But it's really peaceful at night. I like looking at the gravestones and trying to guess whether any of their inhabitants came back as vampires, too. Also, moonlight makes us stronger, which is handy when you have to put up with physics *and* gym the next day. I'm sure vampires back in Transylvania in Wilhelm's day never had to suffer like this.

"If it wasn't one of us," Olympia said, "that would mean there's another vampire in this town." Probably more than one, in fact. We mostly travel in families, just like regular, non-bloodsucking folks. It's easier to blend in that way.

I scanned the growing crowd of students in the parking lot for anyone who looked suspicious. Or, you know . . . hungry.

Mostly everyone just looked sleepy. I mean, it was six o'clock in the morning. Dead body or not, that's way too early for anyone to be awake. I felt that way as a human, and I *definitely* feel that way as a vampire. This is when I should be going to bed and sleeping away all the day-light, but Olympia believes in acting as much like a human as possible. Trust me, I fall asleep the minute I get home from school. I wake up with the darkness and do my homework at three o'clock in the morning.

Most of the faces around us looked tired, like they'd been up late, too.

But there was one guy, though. . . .

Okay, I'll admit it. He caught my attention mostly because he was hot. I mean, sure, I'm a bloodsucking vampire, but I am also still a teenager in a new school; hence, I am always on the lookout for hotties. This one looked like he might be part Japanese, like me. But he had to be part something else, too—maybe Polynesian? Hawaiian?—because his hair was dark and curly, and frankly he looked as if he ought to be surf-ing, or at least starring in a movie about surfing. He was leaning against a black car a few feet away from the police barricade, all casual and whatever: *Oh, look, a murder . . . whatevs.* He had one of those cute little rope necklaces around his neck, and he was wearing sunglasses.

But with my vampire super-sight—all charged

up from last night's moonlit saunter—I could see his eyes through the dark lenses, and that's how I could tell that he was staring intently at the body. It wasn't the *Whoa, dude, there's a dead guy on our steps* kind of staring everyone else was doing.

It was more like *I know exactly what that is.*

Chapter 2

Of course, I'm not a mind reader. Though I hear that's a nifty power which, like mesmerizing people, you can use only after a lot of practice and about a thousand years as a vampire. (Just in case that's true, I'm careful not to think any of my more "degenerate" thoughts around Wilhelm.) So I couldn't be sure what the hot guy's expression meant. But I certainly *wanted* to know.

"Maybe I should go investigate," I said, my hand already on the door handle.

"Wait," Olympia said. "Let's observe for a moment first." I assume her high level of caution is how she's managed to survive seven hundred years, but it drives me bats. (Ha ha ha! More vampire puns! Okay, okay, I'll stop.)

Well, I don't know what *she* was observing,

but *I* kept my "observational" eyes on Mr. Hot. Could he be a vampire? He seemed a lot more tan than me, but maybe he was just born with darker skin.

The problem is that vampires don't look particularly unusual most of the time. I think my canine teeth are maybe a teeny bit longer, but they only get really long and pointy and obvious right before I bite someone. Zach's normal smile, for instance, is toothy and obnoxious, but not in a *Look out! He's going to bite!* kind of way. It's more like *Look out, he's going to hit on you, and then you'll discover that he never flosses!* And if you ask me, dental hygiene should rank pretty high on a vampire's to-do list. Sure, we can't get cavities, but Zach proves that bad breath can be eternal.

Other than his meaty breath, I don't think there are any clues about Zach that would make someone think he's a vampire. He looks like any other doofy seventeen-year-old jock, all muscles and shiny, sandy-blond hair and stupid jokes about body parts. None of that dark, pale, brooding vampire stuff that you read about. He's tall, but that's where the resemblance to Dracula ends.

My new best friend Vivi thinks Zach is *dreamy*, which I find faintly horrifying. (Despite the fact that I once felt the same—which is even *more* horrifying.) But I can't convince her of how wrong she is, because she thinks I'm just like, "Ew, that's my brother," when of course the truth is that he's not my brother at all. And I am *definitely* an expert on his long-term dateability potential.

Zach has no problem with the blood-drinking part of being a vampire, by the way. He mixes it into his morning health shakes with raw eggs and protein powder and all kinds of other unmentionable goop that he says will make him more buff. No one's had the heart to tell him that vampires pretty much stay the same shape they were in when they died. Crystal will never lose that last five pounds; Bert will always look like a teeny-weeny accountant, despite being in reality stronger than any of the men in town. That growth spurt I was sort of hoping for in my senior year is never going to happen—but on the other hand, I can eat as much ice cream and as many cheeseburgers as I want, which I'll admit *almost* makes up for the fact that I still have to drink blood to survive.

Anyway, if I can't even tell that Zach's a vampire, I don't see how I'm supposed to spot a vampire who's a total stranger. I can't exactly walk down the halls of my high school peering at everybody's teeth.

Even with super-sight, I couldn't see anything special about my hot guy's canines, although he did smile helpfully—and very cutely, I might add—at a couple of people who went past him. But once his friends had passed by, he went back to staring at the body in that intense, thoughtful, totally hot way.

"That one," Olympia said suddenly. But she wasn't pointing at my guy. She was pointing at a tall, thin, pale guy in a hooded sweatshirt who was slouching up the sidewalk toward the school. He hadn't even noticed the body yet. His blue eyes were focused on the ground.

I squinted at him. Okay, sure. He was kind of cute, too. In a brooding-poet kind of way. *Or*—I glanced at Olympia—*in a vampire way.* Surely not all pale, brooding guys were secretly vampires, though. Right? I mean, before I died,

I'd known a couple of those quiet, soulful guys in my old school—the ones who never leave the house or cut their hair or speak in class. And *they* weren't vampires. At least, not that I knew of. But Olympia's vampire radar was probably better than mine.

Olympia rolled down her window and pointed at one of the policemen, putting a finger over her lips. I was going to say, "Um, I don't think they can hear us from here," when I realized that now *we* could hear *them* . . . so if anyone out there was a vampire, they'd probably be able to hear us, too. I kept quiet.

The policeman spotted Poet Guy, hurried over to him, and grabbed his elbow.

Poet Guy blinked, finally looking up. "Dad?" His voice was soft, like if moss could talk. He stared around at the crowded parking lot and spotted the body. His expression barely shifted. "Oh. I see."

"Go home, Rowan," his dad said in a low voice.

Rowan shrugged. "Why? It doesn't bother me."

"It *should*," his dad snapped. "I don't want you

near this kind of thing. Go home."

Rowan's eyes narrowed. "Is this because . . . Do you think *I* did this?"

"Of course not. Shut up," the policeman growled, glancing around. He steered Rowan forcefully in a circle and shoved him along the sidewalk until the body was out of sight.

"All right, all right," Rowan said, jerking free. "Not like I care."

"See you at home, son," the policeman said. He wiped his forehead with his sleeve, looking nervous, as he watched Rowan slink away.

I used to like policemen, until they totally failed to save my life. Now every time I see one handing out a parking ticket, I'm like, *Really? You don't have a dying girl to save somewhere? This seems like a better use of your time? Okay, then.*

Olympia rolled up the window again and started the car. It was pretty clear that school was going to be canceled for the day.

"Well spotted," Zach said. "I guess that guy's totally a vampire."

"Perhaps," Olympia said. "Perhaps not. You should keep an eye on him, Kira."

"Me?" I said. "Why me? Can't I keep my eye

on—" I was going to say "that guy instead," but when I turned to point, I realized that my smiley Mr. Hot had vanished. *Sigh*.

"You're on thin ice, Kira," Olympia said. "I suggest you follow the rules as closely as you can until we figure out what happened here."

"I know what happened here," I said. "Some vampire killed Tex Harrison. To be more specific, some vampire who *isn't me*. A not-me vampire who has nothing to do with me."

"Kira!" Olympia said sharply.

"All right, all right," I grumbled, sitting back in my seat and folding my arms mutinously.

Well, fine. It could be worse; at least Rowan was cute in his own way. And after all, I do have two eyes. Nobody said I couldn't also watch Mr. Hot.

Wilhelm had already seen the news on TV by the time we got home. For all that he hates the last thirteen centuries so much, he sure doesn't seem to have a problem with modern technology, most especially TVs. And microwaves to heat your coffee-laced blood. And lights that you can clap on and clap off from the comfort of your own coffin.

"KIRA NOVEMBER!" he hollered from the den as soon as he heard the front door open.

"I DIDN'T DO IT!" I bellowed back.

"YOU GET IN HERE RIGHT NOW!" he shouted. Yeah, in case you were wondering, it turns out that dads are pretty much the same whether they're fifty or fourteen hundred years old.

Olympia put a firm hand on my shoulder before I could dart upstairs. "Let's discuss this," she said meaningfully. *Ugh.* I suppose I should be grateful that I get to be in on these "discussions." My real mom used to just ground me without an explanation or anything, which kind of sucked. But man, Olympia and Wilhelm can talk *forever* about my misbehavior and all the punishments in store for me. I mean, they have all the time in the world—literally. I think most teenagers should count themselves lucky that their parents aren't immortal like mine.

"But I *swear* I didn't do it," I said, trying to fidget away. No luck; Olympia's grip has seven hundred years of vampire strength in it. "What happened to 'innocent until proven guilty'?"

"Doesn't apply to repeat offenders," Zach smirked.

"Shut up, Zach," I said. "Shouldn't Zach have to join us for this? I mean, I don't see why he isn't as suspicious as I am."

"Hello? Alibi?" Zach said, tossing his head annoyingly so his hair resettled in that shiny, perfect way it always does.

"Don't you worry about Zach," Olympia said. She steered me toward the den, and Zach gave me a smug salute as he sauntered up the stairs. "Zach is not your problem, Kira."

But she's wrong about that. Zach is most definitely my problem, and with my luck, he always will be.

Because I'm the one who made him a vampire.

Chapter 3

I met Zach on the first day at my first new school. My previous school, not Luna. It was my first day as a vampire high school student. That was a year ago. Obviously we'd had to move away from my hometown in Michigan; I couldn't exactly keep flitting around Ann Arbor after I'd supposedly died in a car accident. So Olympia relocated us all down South—apparently vampires are used to moving a lot, so no one in the family complained—and signed me up to redo junior year at a new school.

I'd never moved before. I'd lived my whole life in Ann Arbor and always known the same people. Plus I'd never had to deal with hiding a part of my identity before. But I tried to be like, *Okay, so we're in Georgia. I can do this. I'm not just the new girl. I'm a vampire. I don't have to be afraid of mean girls and gossip anymore. I could snap their necks in half—er, not that I will or anything, but it's nice to know that I can. Plus I'm going to live forever. I might as well start acting like it.*

That was the pep talk running through my head for the thousandth time when I finally found my locker that morning, which took a while because there was a guy leaning on it and blocking the number. He grinned down at me. He smelled like testosterone and basketballs.

"Move," I said.

"Ooo, feisty *and* gorgeous," he said, not moving. "Just how I like 'em."

"Ooo, beefy *and* stupid," I said. "Add sweaty and we'll have a trifecta."

"I'll have a trifecta with you anytime," he said, leering. I rolled my eyes. The equally thick-headed guy he was waiting for snickered and closed his locker, which was two over from mine.

"Good one," the thick-headed guy said. "Let's go."

"You go on," Zach said. "I think I'm about to get lucky."

"Yeah, you are," I said. His eyebrows waggled. "Lucky that I don't want to get kicked out,

24

so I'm not going to kill you today."

"Oooooo," Zach said, which maybe should have tipped me off that we'd hit the outer limits of his witty repartee. But just then the bell rang and the hall started to empty, which distracted me.

"Move. *Now.*" I gave him my best steely-eyed vampire glare.

"Or what?" he said, crossing his arms as the last couple of kids hurried into their class-rooms.

"I'm glad you asked," I said. In my head I was like, *You know what, I'm a freaking vampire. I have super-strength, hardly anything can kill me, and if I get in trouble we'll just move again. Why hold back?*

So I threw him into a janitor's closet and locked him in while I went to chemistry.

He was sitting on an overturned bucket when I got back, listening to his iPod. He grinned like a pirate when I opened the door and slipped inside.

"I knew you'd come back," he said.

"You'd have looked pretty silly if I didn't," I said.

"You needed another piece of this pie, didn't

you?" Zach pointed to himself with an *oh, yeah* expression.

"You're much cuter when you don't talk," I said, and kissed him in the dark.

I didn't really mean to encourage his alpha-male obnoxiousness. I mainly wanted to shut him up. And also I wanted to see what would happen. I'd never dated a guy like this. My one and only boyfriend back when I was alive was the sweet, sensitive type who took, like, three years just to ask me out.

Plus, when dealing with a guy like Zach, it was nice to have super-strength. Like, for instance, when I found his hands instantaneously roaming to my butt.

"OW!" he yelped as I flung him into a shelf of toilet paper.

"I make the rules," I said. "Got it? You touch only what I want you to touch."

"Can I have a list?" he said, recovering quickly. "With descriptive details, please?"

"Seriously, shut up," I said. I pushed him into the wall, twisted his hands behind his back, and held them there while I kissed him again. His kisses were very enthusiastic. And he didn't try to free himself, so I figured he'd be easy to train.

He was really warm, and he tasted kind of salty and sweet at the same time. Before I knew what I was doing, my mouth went to his neck. I licked his skin lightly and he shuddered. I could feel my canine teeth sliding out. The blood in his veins pulsed under my tongue.

I realized I wasn't in lust at all. I was *hungry*.

"You," Zach whispered in my ear, "are the hottest, most psycho girl I've ever met."

His voice stopped me just before my teeth grazed his skin. What was I doing?

I dropped his hands and jumped away from him as if he had holy water running through his veins. Olympia had warned me that it would be hard once I was around mortals all day long, especially attractive, young mortals. But it didn't even occur to me that kissing could lead so quickly to wanting to bite someone. Especially someone whom I did not by any means want to turn into a vampire.

That was one of the rules Olympia had lectured me about over and over again: "You bite it, you bought it." We were responsible for anyone we turned into a vampire. That's how we survive. If we let new vampires wander loose with no idea of the rules, they'd be staked in no time, and the rest of the world would soon catch on that we exist.

It is possible to bite someone and leave them alive, but it's dangerous and hard to do—Olympia says once you start to drink, it's almost impossible to stop yourself before your prey is dead. And even if you do stop, the victim probably will have figured out what you are, and that's not great for us either.

I was lucky that Zach couldn't see my teeth in the darkness of the closet. I covered my face and tried to force them back down to normal. *Don't think about feeding. Don't think about feeding.*

"Wait," Zach said, groping for me with his hands outstretched. "Don't stop. What happened?"

"I lost interest," I said, stepping out of his reach. My fingers were trembling, but I kept my voice level. "Too bad for you. Now stay away from my locker." And I got out of there as quickly as I could.

I probably should have guessed that this wouldn't shut down Zach. If anything, it made him even more interested. I started finding him at my locker every morning when I got there, usually with chocolate. My guess is, he read in some men's magazine that girls like chocolate, because he really stuck with that theory.

I ignored him for the first week. He loved it when I shoved him out of my way; he went on and on about how freakishly strong I was "for such a tiny thing," until it started making me nervous. I was sure Olympia didn't want to hear gossip about the new freakishly strong teenager while she was buying up all the raw meat in the supermarket.

So at first I started talking to Zach just to distract him. I told him if he really wanted to bring me something before class, he should try hot chocolate and a croissant. That fit his theory just fine, so the next morning, there was my order, exactly as I'd requested. Like I said—the early signs pointed to "easily trainable."

"Hmm," I said, letting the hot chocolate scald away the taste of blood on my tongue.

"So you'll go out with me this weekend,

right?" Zach asked. "I figured we could start with dinner at Los Espejos." He pronounced it "ezz-PAY-joes," but I still recognized it as the Spanish word for *mirrors*. Olympia and Wilhelm had scouted out all the more dangerous places in town, and this Spanish restaurant was at the top of the list. It was lovely and expensive, but the walls and the ceiling were completely covered in mirrors. Too risky, no matter how besotted my date might be. Our little "family" tried to avoid even walking past it.

"*Meh*," I said with a shrug. "I'd rather have a hamburger at Big Burgers and Bowling."

He clutched his heart. "You *are* my dream girl."

So that's how it started. And I'll admit it: I kind of fell for him. Dating Zach fit the new take-no-prisoners attitude I was trying to develop. I figured if I could be a badass vampire, I wouldn't miss my old life so much. It was nice having someone to distract me from wishing I could call my mom or kiss Jeremy one last time.

Plus it was sort of exciting to have someone be *that* into me. He couldn't keep his hands off me, no matter how many times I threw him into a wall or nearly broke his fingers. I admired his persistence.

On the other hand, it got harder and harder not to bite him. You have to understand, the blood we drink every day to stay alive comes out of a jar in the refrigerator. It is the very definition of gross. Vampires are designed to drink from living (or very recently dead) people; that's what we're hungry for. Olympia was trying to teach me to exercise self-control, but I wasn't learning nearly fast enough to keep up with my relationship with Zach.

After three months, I started thinking about the future. By that point, I thought Zach was pretty hot. I figured it was almost definitely true love forever. And wouldn't it suck (ha ha!) if I stayed sixteen and he got older and older? Wouldn't it make more sense to turn him into a vampire while he was still my own age? Then we could really be together forever. Awesome, right?

But I still don't think I would have done anything on my own. I would have waited at *least* another three months to be sure that I liked him that much. I mean, I'm not *totally* crazy.

Unfortunately, it was only a month later when Zach spotted my teeth sliding out during one of our make-out sessions—this time in a closet that was apparently not dim enough.

"Whoa," he said, stepping back. "What's wrong with your teeth?"

"Uh—nothing," I said, covering my mouth with one hand. I turned away from him, but he grabbed my arm and pulled me around.

"That is so weird," he said, which was a much calmer reaction than I would have had. He reached out and touched one of my teeth with his index finger. A drop of blood immediately appeared on his skin, and I panicked. Was that enough to turn him into a vampire? That wouldn't be fair! I hadn't *intentionally* bitten him!

At the same time, I couldn't stop myself from licking it off. He took his hand back and we stared at each other for a minute.

"Okay, yes," I said. "I'm a vampire."

Zach let out a bark of laughter. "That's impossible," he said.

I let my teeth slide all the way out and held

back my hair so he could see the marks on my neck. "It's not impossible; it's just lame. Here, check for a pulse, you'll see." I grabbed his hand and wrapped his fingers around my wrist.

I knew he wouldn't find a heartbeat on me, but we were close enough to each other that I could hear his own heart speeding up as he held my wrist and stared at me some more.

"Don't worry," I said. "I don't bite. Ha ha." I took my hand back, prying off his fingers. I was about to walk out of there and straight home to tell Olympia we needed to move again, when he finally spoke, in a wobbly, *I just saw a pterodactyl* kind of voice.

"What if I wanted you to?" he asked.

"Wanted me to what?"

"Bite me," he said. He took my wrists again and pulled me closer, shaking back his hair to expose his neck. "Do it. I want to be like you. I want to be a vampire, too."

"Yikes, dude," I said, trying not to look at his neck. "Care to think about that for half a minute? It's kind of like proposing to me, only even *more* eternal." I thought that would scare him off, but it didn't. Which maybe should have been a warning sign, but at the time I found it endearing. So sue me. I was in love . . . or at least I thought I was.

"Exactly," Zach said. "I love you. I'll always love you. I want to be with you forever."

I didn't say yes. Not even with his neck right there waiting for me. Some little corner of my brain was going, *Wait! Think! This is not a normal reaction! Run away!* Unfortunately that little voice wasn't yelling loud enough, although it tried its best for the next few weeks, during which Zach pleaded with me *every day* to turn him into a vampire. Even in my love-blind state, I started to find it pretty annoying. I kept thinking, *Can we please have* one date *that doesn't end with you shoving your neck in my face and pledging your undying love? Can't we just eat pizza and maybe talk about our homework now and then?*

Then one day he called me and told me to come over right away. I told him it would have to wait because I was dyeing my hair. He told me he was dying.

I said, "You too? What color?"

And he said, "No, seriously dying. I mean *dying*."

"Literally?" I said. "Could you wait until my hair is dry?"

He said he didn't think so, because there was a lot of blood already, more than he'd expected.

That's when I realized he was serious.

Thank goodness for vampire super-speed. I got to his house in about nine seconds flat. And sure enough, the moron had slit his own wrists.

"What did you do?" I yelled at him. He was lying in the bathtub, looking pale, as blood pooled around his jeans and bare chest.

"I did it . . . for you," he said in this whispery, trying-to-be-heroic voice.

"You are the world's biggest idiot. What if I hadn't been home? What if I'd been in the shower? You might have been dead before I even knew what you'd done. Which would have served you right, numbskull."

"Well, I didn't want you to stop me," he said, sounding irritated and a little less whispery. "And don't call me an idiot."

The scent of all the fresh blood was making me dizzy. "We should wrap you up," I said, "and get you to a hospital." I grabbed a towel and knelt next to the tub.

"It's too late for that," he said, back to his dying voice. He practically pressed the back of his hand to his forehead. "I'm dying, Kira. You have to change me . . . to save me."

"I should have left you in that closet on the first day," I snapped. I took his nearest wrist and started to wrap the towel around the wounds. The blood soaked through the white cloth instantly, spreading like red fireworks.

Zach lifted his wrist toward my face, and the towel fell off with a *splat*. "Drink," he said. "It's all right. I want you to. Then we can be together . . . forever."

There was nothing else I could do. The smell of all that blood was too much for my willpower. I was sure I'd never get him to the hospital in time. He was going to die, and it would be my fault.

I sank my fangs into the bloody gouges on his arms.

Yeah, it was amazing. It was the last amazing moment I had with Zach. I don't want to describe it, because remembering it now makes me feel all creepy, but it was mind-blowing. I can see how some vampires become addicted to drinking from the living. Olympia had warned me about that, too.

After Zach was fully dead, I left his body there and went home to tell Olympia what had happened. She laughed and laughed and laughed until she literally fell out of her coffin. Which, incidentally, was not quite the reaction I was expecting.

"Well, we're in love," I said, offended. "I'm sure it'll turn out fine. Like Bert and Crystal."

"Oh, dear," Olympia said, wiping tears from her eyes. "Now perhaps you'll see why listening to seven hundred years of experience is a good idea."

Yeah. About a month later, in a rental car somewhere in the middle of Kansas, while we were moving around every night to hide our trail, Zach tried to get to second base with me and I threw him out of the sun roof. We had to drive half a mile back to find him. He sulked all the way to Montana.

That was the end of that relationship.

Chapter 4

Tragically, I am now stuck with Zach until he decides to go off and start his own vampire family somewhere, which requires a level of maturity I'm fairly sure he won't be able to muster anytime in the next five hundred years.

On the plus side, our cover story in this new town was that we were supposed to be brother and sister, so he couldn't hit on me in public anymore. That didn't stop him from trying sometimes when we were at home—hence the long midnight walks to avoid him. He kept staring soulfully into my eyes and saying things like, "You want to be with me, Kira," or "We are meant for each other," which would maybe have more impact if his idea of "soulful" didn't involve enormous, googly eyeballs. The good news is,

I'm still a lot stronger than him, as apparently that is a skill I am extra-blessed with. Zach? Not so much. Olympia has asked me to stop throwing him out windows, though. They're expensive to replace and the noise might disturb the neighbors.

That whole saga is why they immediately blamed me for this new vampire attack. As if I hadn't learned my lesson! I was pretty sure I'd never date again, just in case I accidentally landed another obsessive lunatic. If you asked me, I was the vampire *least* likely to bite another high school football player.

But Wilhelm was convinced that after biting Zach, I'd become addicted.

"I knew this would happen!" he huffed, wagging his finger in the air. "I knew it was foolish to turn a child of this horrifying century! She's a degenerate menace! We should lock her in a coffin and feed her through a tube until she is old enough to be trusted!"

I glanced at Olympia. "You guys don't really do that, do you?"

"Not unless it's necessary," Olympia said, which didn't reassure me very much.

We were in the den, which is Wilhelm's favorite room after the basement, where he sleeps. Olympia deliberately chose a house with very few windows—they're hard to find, but cheap, because nobody else wants them. The den had only one small window. Like all the others in the house, it was covered with dark blinds *and* heavy velvet curtains.

On the table next to Wilhelm's Barcalounger was the only light in the room: a tiny lamp with a pale red shade. Olympia had convinced Wilhelm to give up his dripping, Gothic candles after he set the last Barcalounger on fire. This new chair was covered in a prickly red-and-black plaid. The colors matched the dark red Oriental rug and the sleek, black metal coffee table, but stylistically the room was a bit of a mishmash.

My vampire parents are not exactly the world's greatest interior decorators. It's like they've latched onto a couple of trendy things from each century and haven't noticed that the world has moved on. This is unfortunately true of their clothes, too. We're not even going to discuss the tragedy of a medieval vampire in a pale blue leisure suit. I make Olympia run her outfits by me every morning befo   to school.

"She is running wild!" W
now, talking about me again. "
the vampire hunters right to us!"

"This isn't the Dark Ages, Pops,"   said. I
love the way Wilhelm's hair stands on end when
I call him that. "There aren't mobs of ignorant
villagers outside with pitchforks and torches.
Nobody even believes you guys exist. Us guys,
I mean."

"That is precisely the kind of thinking that
will get us all staked!" he shouted. "These new
vampires think they can bite anyone they like!
They don't remember how the hunters watch for
any signs of us! Careless, reckless, selfish—"

"But *I didn't do it*!" I yelled over the end of his
sentence. "Call me what you like, but I DIDN'T
BITE HIM!"

Wilhelm glared at me with beady, bloodshot
eyes. He wasn't bitten until fairly late in life, so
he's kind of grizzled and gray for a vampire.
Plus he's had the same moustache since the
800s—long and droopy and fluffy. Apparently
it keeps going in and out of fashion, so he sees

o shave it. Personally I think it's really
stracting to talk to someone who looks like he
has giant, fuzzy caterpillars crawling out of his
nose.

"It might be true," Olympia interjected. "We
can't be sure she did it."

"We can't be sure she *didn't*," Wilhelm snarled.
"We should move again, and quickly, before they
come to hunt us down."

"Oh, *no*," I said, remembering the long weeks
of car travel and switching cities and identities.
It was bad enough after my death; after Zach's
it was even worse, because he was there pester-
ing me the whole time and there was no way to
get away from him. I was kind of hoping we'd
stay here in Massachusetts for a while. "*Please*
don't make me start junior year all over again."

"I hardly think relocating is the worst of your
problems," Olympia pointed out.

"There could *totally* be other vampires here,"
I said. "We saw this *way* suspicious guy at the
school, didn't we, Olympia? And it's a pretty big
town, right? There could be vampires all over
the place!"

"Most vampires are not as foolish as you

are," Wilhelm growled.

"Let me find the vampire who killed Tex," I said. "If I can figure out who did it, will you believe me? Can we stay?"

Olympia and Wilhelm looked at each other for a long moment. Sometimes I think they're actually talking to each other when this happens, which is fully creepy. Nobody wants parents with telepathy.

Finally Wilhelm snorted, which made his moustache flounce up and down. "I am not happy about this," he said. "I want that to be clear."

"All right, we'll let you try," Olympia said to me. "But if you haven't figured it out in one week, we're moving again."

"And then there *will* be consequences," Wilhelm warned. I didn't need telepathy to know he had locked coffins and feeding tubes floating through his head.

"Be careful," Olympia said. "Not all vampires are as civilized as we are."

Really? Less civilized than medieval Romanians? I bet.

Finally I escaped upstairs to my room. Zach

and I are the only ones who use the upstairs; we don't quite hate the sun as much as the others do, and it occasionally manages to sneak in through the blinds on the top floor. Our deal is that I get the rooms to the left of the staircase and he gets the rooms to the right. He's not supposed to come over to my side, although you can imagine how well he obeys that rule.

Bert and Crystal have a room on the first floor. They've both been vampires for less than a hundred years, so they still do some human things like sleep in a bed, although their mattress is rock hard. I guess one day they'll switch over to coffins, like Olympia and Wilhelm, who sleep behind a hidden door in the basement in parallel caskets of ancient stone. Allegedly one day I'll want to sleep in a coffin, too, but I am *highly* dubious about that theory. I like my bed to be as fluffy as possible, with about seventeen pillows and a down comforter. Wilhelm thinks this is a sign of my "moral decrepitude" and "debilitating laziness." I think it's a sign of *I just like sleeping, dude.*

In fact, when I got upstairs, that's exactly what happened—pretty much right away. I mean, I *tried* to start my investigation. I got as far as Googling *Tex Harrison* and finding out that he kept a blog on his MySpace page. But it turned out to be all about sports and how awesome the Luna Tigers are and what an awesome quarterback he is and *blah blah* Patriots and Red Sox, plus a detailed rundown of his daily workout regimen and everything he's ever eaten. Ever. Can you really blame me for falling asleep?

When I woke up, I was lying across my bed in a mountain of pillows. My vampire instincts told me that it was dark outside. I rolled over and saw Zach standing in my doorway. Really, "lurking" is the most appropriate description.

"Go away," I said, throwing a pillow at him.

"You forgot to lock your door again," he said.

"*You* forgot to not be an ass again," I said. "Stay on your side of the house."

"I hear you're going to solve Tex's murder," he said with a smirk. "Looks like it's going well so far."

"Um, hello? All the best detectives do their work in the dark," I said.

"I can think of better things to do in the

dark," he said, waggling his eyebrows.

That was my cue to leave.

"Have some blood before you go out!" Olympia called from the kitchen as I stomped past.

"No, thanks!" I called back, grabbing my keys. I slammed the door behind me and started running. I never used to like running, but it turns out it's a lot more fun when you're nearly as fast as a car. And it doesn't make me tired anymore, at least as long as the moon is out. Plus it's a lot safer to run unnaturally fast at night— not so many people out on the street.

I made it to the high school in about ten minutes. It looked all gloomy and shadowy in the moonlight, the brick and concrete merging into silvery edges. Most of the glass had been swept up, but I could see a few tiny shards they'd missed still shimmering on the steps. I guess the police had been busy, because even the crime scene tape was gone. They probably really wanted school to get back to normal the next day.

They'd done a pretty good job of cleaning up; only the smell of blood still lingered, a whisper of what had happened here, and I'm guessing that only a vampire nose would pick that up. Even the broken window above was covered with a black tarp, one corner flapping a little in the wind.

There's another cemetery right beside the high school—not the one I usually go to. This one is smaller and older, with tiny, crooked gravestones. With that on one side and the football field on the other, the school has a lot of open space around it. Only a couple of houses have a view of the front steps, and that's across the parking lot. I was guessing nobody could have seen anything, especially that late at night, without vampire sight. It was only eleven o'clock now, and already all the houses were dark. Unhelpful day-dwellers.

I padded across the grass that edged the parking lot, staying close to the shadows just in case. Long trails of purple-gray clouds slid across the moon. A small piece of glass crunched under my sneaker as I climbed the steps. Tex must have landed with a lot of force; I could smell blood spatters on the front door. And blood was the only thing I could smell. The scent of the attacker was completely masked by the over-whelming scent of Tex's blood.

The door was, of course, locked, which made me wonder how Tex and his killer had gotten inside in the middle of the night in the first place.

Not that it's hard for a vampire to get into places like this. We have to be invited into private homes, but everything else is wide open to us. For instance, I could have just pulled the door off, but I thought that might be a little suspicious. Probably not an approach Olympia would have approved of.

Instead I climbed the big oak tree that grows beside the school's front steps. Climbing trees is another thing that's more fun with vampire strength and speed. I was level with the top floor in about twenty seconds. I wriggled along the length of a branch until I could reach the flapping corner of the tarp. There was just enough space for me to squeeze underneath and flip through the open window. The broken panes of glass were gone. Only a gaping round hole was left in the wall of the school.

My shoes hit the tile floor with a tiny squeak.

I was in a long hallway lined with metallic-green junior class lockers. Moonlight slanted through the windows in the classrooms on either side and the matching round window at the far end of the hall, facing the back of the school. Another hallway bisected this one in the middle, making a kind of plus sign. Or a cross, if you want to be all *woooooo* mystical about it. As it turns out, crosses don't bother me. They freak Wilhelm out really badly, though, so I think maybe you had to believe in them when you were alive to be bothered by them once you're a vampire. I would test this theory by throwing a Star of David at Bert, but that would be mean.

Holy water does irritate my skin, and garlic makes me sneeze for about an hour. Neither of them can kill me, though—so much for those theories. I'm afraid it's a stake through the heart, an axe through the neck, or a whole lot of fire, and that's it. Not stuff I have to worry about much in my everyday life. Unlife. Whatever.

I circled the spot in the hallway in front of the open window, although I had no idea what I was looking for. Clues? Graffiti scrawled on

49

the wall: "I killed Tex Harrison here"? The floor looked as scuffed and ordinary as it did every day. I crouched and ran my hand across the cold, speckled tiles.

My fingers brushed against something that rolled. I caught it and picked it up.

A small red bead.

Hmmmmm.

Of course, anyone could have dropped that here anytime. Hundreds of kids went through this hall every day. My own locker was right around the corner, in the bisecting hallway.

Still, I slipped the bead into my pocket.

Although I knew it wouldn't do any good, I inhaled, trying to see if any of the scents here were stronger than the others. As I expected, there was too much of a jumble to pick anything out.

Except . . . No, I was wrong. There was *one* unusually sharp scent. It's hard to describe how vampire noses distinguish what they smell, but if it helps, this one smelled a little like mist and moonlight and jazz and tuxedos and antique books. (I know, I bet that was really helpful.)

As I separated it out from the rest of the

muddle, I realized that it was surprisingly strong and getting stronger.

Or . . . closer.

I whirled around.

I wasn't alone.

Chapter 5

$\mathcal{I}$f I'd *had* a heartbeat, it would have skidded to a stop.

He was standing in the doorway of a classroom, his hands clasped behind his back. The moonlight dappled the floor behind him, hiding his face in shadow. All I could see was his long, lean outline.

I was pretty sure he was staring at me.

A long moment passed. He didn't move. I didn't move. Oh, I *thought* about moving. I thought about leaping right out that broken window. I figured the fall wouldn't hurt me too badly, and then I could run all the way home.

But he probably had seen my face already, so it would be a bad idea to do anything vampire-y right now—like, say, survive a three-story fall.

Anyway, I couldn't have moved if I'd wanted to. I was way too freaking scared. He just *stood* there. He had this eerie stillness about him that I'd never seen before. I couldn't even hear him breathing or fidgeting or anything. The hallway was completely silent. Just me and a sinister figure in the dark.

Kira, you're a vampire, I told myself. *He should be scared of you. What's he going to do to you? Is it worse than being locked in a coffin and fed through a feeding tube for a hundred years?*

But the other half of my brain was merrily reminding me that criminals often return to the scene of the crime, while gory pictures of Tex's bleeding corpse flashed across my mental movie screen. Tex, who had been killed by a *vampire*.

My mind started racing again. *Do vampires kill other vampires? How would he do it? IS HE HIDING A STAKE BEHIND HIS BACK?*

When he finally did move, I nearly leaped out of my skin. All he did was take a tiny step forward, but it startled me enough that I jumped backward, crashed into the lockers behind me, slipped on the floor, and fell over.

So much for the preternatural grace of vampires. I'd love to know when *that's* finally going to kick in.

And then, all at once, he was right beside me.

"I'm sorry," he said, kneeling next to me as I sat up. "I didn't mean to scare you."

"Really?" I said. "You're just *naturally* that terrifying?"

Now that he was out in the hall, I could see his face, but that didn't help because I'd never seen him before. He looked like he was my age, with coffee-colored skin and close-cropped, curly black hair and a dancer's body, which I mention only because his shirt was open and I could see his abs above his jeans, and these were *definitely* abs worth mentioning.

I found myself thinking, *Wow, I* hope *he's a vampire!* I mean, not that I knew anything about vampire-vampire dating, but it had to be less complicated than dating a human, right? Unless he was the killer vampire. Hot or not, I don't date murderers.

"You startled me," he said, with a hint of a smile. His voice matched his scent, sort of moody and layered, like he would have fit in perfectly as a saxophone player in an underground 1920s jazz club.

"Uh, no," I said. "*You* startled *me*."

"I did," he said. "I apologize." The unspoken question hung in the air between us. *What the hell are you doing here?* I would have asked, but I was trying to come up with a good answer myself. Plus I was a little distracted by how perfectly shaped his eyes were. If Michelangelo and Rembrandt and the top casting directors in Hollywood all got together to design the perfect face, they'd probably start with this guy's eyes. It was kind of impossible not to gaze dreamily into them.

"I'm Daniel," he said.

"I'm Kira," I said, although in my daze I nearly slipped and told him my real name, from back when I was a human. "Do you go to school here?"

And then he took my hands in his and helped me to my feet.

Wait, let me go over that one more time.

His long, elegant hands slid over mine, gripped my fingers gently, and lifted me up in such a smooth motion that I was standing before

I'd even had time to recover from the softness and strength of his hands.

Which is why I nearly missed his answer—but seriously, right then his hands seemed a lot more important than anything he could possibly say.

"I'm new. Tomorrow's my first day," he said, and he let go of my hands. Which was disappointing, but it sure seemed like he'd held them a moment longer than necessary . . . hadn't he?

"Oh," I said. "Tomorrow. Wow." Yeah. There were many things about this situation that were short-circuiting my ability to form sentences.

"Yes," he said. "Not quite the welcome I was expecting." He made a small gesture toward the window, which reminded us both that we were standing in the midst of a murder scene in the middle of the night. We stared at each other again for a long moment.

I broke first. "Oh," I said, like it had just occurred to me, "you must think it's so weird that I'm here, don't you?" Implied: *Because* I *think it's pretty weird that* you're *here*. I laughed nervously. "Okay, this is going to sound crazy, but I . . . needed a book from my locker."

He cocked one elegant eyebrow at me. "A book?"

"Yeah," I said. "Shakespeare. *Macbeth.* Very gloomy. Lots of mu—" *Don't say murder!* "—umbling. Mumbling about . . . witches . . . and stuff. Have you read it?" *Oh, that was suave. Clever* and *romantic, all in one fell swoop.*

"A long time ago," he said with a half smile.

"Well, we have a test tomorrow, and I have to finish reading it, so I thought I'd get it now." I trailed off lamely, wondering how much he had seen of me climbing through the window and searching the floor.

"Oh," he said. "Of course. I'd have thought they'd cancel any tests scheduled for tomorrow, but it's always wise to be prepared."

"Yeah," I said. "That's me! Prepared." For tests, yes. For strange, hot boys in moonlit hallways, not so much.

There was another pause. Two could play this little game. I lifted an eyebrow at *him.*

He laughed softly. "All right. I have a confession to make."

Score! Murder solved! Well, that was much easier than I'd expected. Wilhelm and Olympia would be so proud. Assuming I made it out of here alive. Well, you know . . . "alive."

"I heard about the murder," Daniel said, gesturing again, "and I'm afraid I was curious. I thought I should know more about my new school. I like figuring things out myself . . . I guess you could say I'm an amateur detective." He rubbed his head, looking convincingly sheepish. "Do you think I'm terribly strange now?"

Yes, but don't worry, the "terribly hot" part makes up for it. I couldn't figure out whether he was lying. It sounded about as believable as my story—which is to say, not very.

"No," I lied. "I bet lots of other students would have done it if they could have figured out how to get in. Um . . . how did you get in?"

"Through the boys' locker room," Daniel said, pointing down. "The lock was already broken, so I just walked in."

HMMMMMMM.

Possibility one: Daniel was lying, and he'd broken the lock himself to get in, which he could easily do if he were a vampire.

Possibility two: Some other vampire, possibly of the murderous variety, had broken the lock earlier this evening to come up here and revisit the crime scene, as I hear criminals do all the time.

Possibility three: That's how Tex got in last night—as did the vampire who killed him.

"Isn't that how you got in?" Daniel said innocently.

"Um, yeah," I said. "Of course. Lucky break for me."

He glanced at my hands. "So . . . where's the book?"

"I was just going to get it," I said, trying to look all casual. He followed me down the hall and around the corner to my locker. I laughed awkwardly. "I guess I wanted to look at the crime scene, too."

"A fellow investigator," he said with that hint of a smile again.

I rummaged through my messy locker until I found *Macbeth*. The clang of the door closing echoed way too loudly along the empty hall. Daniel and I both went really quiet for a moment, as if he was also listening to be sure we were alone in the school.

"Let's get out of here," he whispered. He led

the way to the nearest stairwell, and we padded softly down to the bottom floor. I noticed that he didn't seem hesitant about where to go—he led the way straight through the last door, turned left, and headed right for the locker room. Either he had a good sense of direction, or he knew this school better than he was letting on.

I'd never been in a boys' locker room before, not even when I was dating Zach, king of high school athletics back in Georgia. To put it politely, the smell was much . . . stronger . . . than in the girls' locker room. Daniel chivalrously held the door open for me, so I had a chance to glance around when we first went in. I spotted a row of mirrors over the sinks, off in an alcove. Wouldn't it be useful if I could spot Daniel in one of those . . . or not spot him, as the case may be—if, say, it turned out he had no reflection? But getting any closer would run the risk that he'd notice *my* lack of reflection, too.

I watched him as he wove through the benches. Was he avoiding the mirrors like I was? If he was, he was pretty casual about it. We made it to the door that led onto the football field, and I checked out the broken lock. It looked like a super-strength job—as if someone had just grabbed the door and pulled, snapping the lock mechanism in half.

Outside, the clouds were clearing up, and rays of moonlight sliced across the football field in front of us. Daniel paused in an oval of silver light and looked down at me.

"It was nice to meet you, Kira," he said.

"Yeah, you, too. Welcome to the school," I added wryly. "It's usually not quite this exciting. Um—I mean awful. Well, okay, it's usually awful, but in a different, really boring way. Um, but I'm sure you'll love it." *Okay, stop talking now.*

"I'm looking forward to it a lot more now that I've met you," he said. A slow smile spread across his face. It was a sexy smile, a candles-and-black-lace smile—the polar opposite of Zach's dopey *let's do it in a closet* leer.

"See you tomorrow, then," I said, smiling back.

He touched his forehead in a little salute and started to walk away across the football field.

"Daniel," I called after he'd gone a couple of paces. He turned and looked at me, walking backward. "Did you find anything upstairs? I mean—about the murder?"

He smiled the same smile again, but for some reason, this time it sent chills down my spine.

"Oh," he said. "I have some theories."

Then the moon went behind another cloud, and when it emerged again, Daniel was gone.

Chapter 6

$\mathcal{I}$ spent the rest of the night trying to make lists of clues to help me solve the mystery. To give you an idea of how well that went, here's what my "Daniel" list looked like:

DANIEL
* *Hot*
* *Likes hanging out at murder scenes at night*
* *Really hot*
* *Says he wants to be a detective*
* *Great abs*
* *Starting school right after the murder— suspicious?*
* *Extremely, totally, remarkably hot*

And here's another list:

SMILEY GUY

* *Looked at the crime scene v. suspiciously*
* *Also very hot*
* *Where have these hot boys been hiding?*
* *Too smiley to be a vampire?*
* *Really cute smile*
* *Find out name . . . investigate further . . .*
  critically important: great abs or not?
* *Like,* seriously *cute smile*

So it wasn't exactly Nancy Drew–caliber work. Perhaps you can tell that I'd been stuck with Zach for the last six months of moving and hiding and *not* meeting hot new guys, so I was having some side effects. I don't normally obsess over abs that much. At least I don't think I do. Then again, my experience with hot-guy abs is fairly limited so far. Presumably in, like, a century or so, I'll be all blasé: *Oh yeah, abs, whatever—been there, done that.*

I checked Tex's blog again to see what the last entry said. Scrolling back, I saw that he usually posted twice a day—once in the morning to record his breakfast and morning workout, and once in the evening to talk about what else he'd eaten, how totally kickass he was, and what sports he'd watched that day. He'd posted the last entry on the morning of the day he died.

It said:

Toaster waffles, bacon, and a protein shake for breakfast. Measured my biceps again—still the same as yesterday's. LAME. Think I'll go for another swim before school. Just because I quit the now totally loser-filled swim team doesn't mean I have to stay out of the pool, right? I feel like shooting some hoops this afternoon. That'd be good for my biceps, right? Huh. Still hungry. Maybe I'll see if there's any leftover pizza in the fridge. Go Sox!

Well, that told me nothing, although it did make me hungry. Birds were starting to twitter outside, and the pale blue light coming through my blinds told me it was dawn. I hid my clue sheets in my desk and went downstairs to ferret out some breakfast. Breakfast in a vampire household . . . let's just say: *Sigh*.

Okay, brace yourselves for a really hilarious joke here: Being a vampire sucks. Ahahahaha,

I know, so clever. I bet you've never heard that before.

But seriously? It *sucks*.

For one thing, I used to be a vegetarian. I mean, I'd been a vegetarian for only, like, four months when I was turned, but still. I had to go directly from "Peace, haters! Cows are our friends! Let the chickens live! Fish deserve rights!" to "Oh, yes, thanks, I would love another gallon of blood for lunch. Yum."

Also, blood is disgusting.

I used to make myself drink a glass of orange juice every day because I thought it was good for me and it would help me live longer (ha ha ha ha . . . ha), even though I hated the taste. *Well*. Right now I would give anything to *drown in an ocean of orange juice* rather than have to take another sip of disgusting, cold, ooky pig's blood.

But I have no choice. We need blood every day to live. I literally have to choke down at least two glasses of blood every morning, just to make it through the day.

I've tried disguising it in lots of creative ways, the way my vampire family does—in milkshakes or on top of ice cream (highly not recommended) or scrambled into an omelet or baked into pancakes. But it is *still blood* and it is *awful* and plus then the pancakes or ice cream or eggs are totally ruined. So now I just hold my nose, pour it down, and eat as much as I can of something else afterward to get rid of the taste.

In the old days, vampires got their blood from people, of course. It's a lot more exciting and it tastes much better that way, and a vampire needs to do that only about once a month to survive. But it's hard to be subtle about six vampires feeding in one town once a month, plus, if we start, Olympia is sure we won't be able to stop. So instead she sends Bert out on blood runs to towns that are at least two to four hours away to buy animal blood in bulk, which just barely sustains us and is also completely disgusting.

When I got downstairs, Olympia was rummaging in the fridge and Crystal was slicing tomatoes. Bert was sitting at the kitchen island, pouring blood into his cereal bowl. His horn-rimmed glasses were perched on his nose, and he was peering at the *Wall Street Journal*. Bert and Olympia manage our finances in some mysterious way that involves shadow companies and long-held stocks and stakes in lots of big corporations (obviously not *those* kinds of stakes), so we have plenty of money and none of the adult vampires have to work if they don't want to.

I'm sure I'll appreciate that once I'm done with high school and I can live a charming life of leisure, too. But right now I just picture them sleeping peacefully all day while I suffer through band in a hot music room that smells like sweaty marching uniforms, and it makes me wildly jealous.

I sat down and stared gloomily at the blood going *gloop-gloop-gloop* over Bert's cornflakes.

"It's *grrrrrrrrrrrrrrrrrrrr-oss*!" I joked.

Of course, nobody got my brilliant Tony the Tiger reference, because none of these people have ever watched enough television. Bert gave me a puzzled look and then went back to his paper.

My mom would have laughed. I can't believe I miss her.

"Hey, Kira," Crystal said brightly. "Olympia says you're solving a mystery!" Crystal was twenty when she died, in 1926—I'm not sure how, because in my house, we don't talk about how we died. Except for Zach, who *ought* to be embarrassed about it but apparently isn't, since he brings it up incessantly. I was surprised when he remembered all the details of his death; I barely remember anything about the car accident that killed me.

Anyway, it's a good thing Crystal got to stick around for the sixties, because that was the perfect decade for her. I think she's hoping it'll come back sometime. She still wears tie-dyed shirts and bell-bottoms as often as she can. She has pale blond hair that curls around her chin, and she likes to come into my room and dance in the middle of the night, no matter what music I'm listening to. She'll dance to anything. As vampire sisters go, she's not bad. Certainly better than Apolla, the very quiet little sister I had when I was alive. She was ten when I died and was known around our house as "the good one."

Crystal is my favorite member of my new family. Although the early morning perkiness—actually, the *all-the-time* perkiness—is probably going to get old after a couple of decades.

"Yup," I said. "A mystery. *Wheeee.*"

Crystal found Bert sometime during the Great Depression and turned him into a vampire after they fell in love. This turned out much better for her than it did for me with Zach. Which is sort of mysterious, since Bert is a buttoned-up math nerd and Crystal is a ditzy free spirit. I never would have put them together, but here we are, like, seventy years later, and unfortunately they still act schmoopy around each other all the time.

Crystal dropped a kiss on Bert's head as she sat down with us. Her morning blood was spread on three toasted tomato sandwiches. I couldn't even look at them.

Olympia plunked a tall glass of blood on the island beside me. "Are you sure you don't want me to heat it for you?" she asked, like she does every morning.

"No, thanks," I said. It might taste more like living blood that way, but when it's hot I can't drink it as fast and get it over with.

"Where are you going to start?" Crystal asked me, bubbling with excitement. "Do you

have a list of suspects? Are you going to inter-
rogate them?"

"Don't forget the one we saw yesterday,"
Olympia said.

"Rowan something," I said. "I know. I thought
I'd try to meet him today. Crystal, would you
help me with my makeup?"

"Oooo, yes!" Crystal chirped, bouncing up
and down.

Not having a reflection anymore is a huge
pain in the butt. *You* try getting ready for
high school every morning with no mirror.
I've mostly given up on wearing makeup these
days; otherwise I'd have to wake up Crystal
every morning to do it for me. It's pretty difficult to put on eyeliner when you can't even
tell where your eyes *are*. But I figured that
on this occasion it would be helpful to be as
cute as possible—you know, if I was going to
subtly investigate cute boys. Not for flirting
purposes, of course. Just for clue-finding and
mystery-solving, yes, sir.

The good news is, I can still see my clothes,
although in the mirror they kind of look like
they're floating in space, which is not always

helpful. Yes, a vampire has no reflection, but our clothes still do. I mean, why would our *clothes* suddenly not show up in mirrors? Wouldn't that be weird? It's not like anybody sucked all the blood out of my *sweaters* or anything.

The same is true for anything we put on ourselves—earrings, makeup, et cetera. For instance, Olympia recommends that we all dye our hair regularly. The fake color shows up in mirrors, which is enough to trick most people. If, out of the corner of their eyes, they catch clothes and hair going by in a mirror, they probably won't notice the missing face and hands.

Of course, I think Olympia was picturing a nice brown or blond or even red for me. She dyes her own hair black, which if you ask me is a little cliché.

Me? I went for green.

Not bright, crazy, Kermit green or anything. I have pretty dark hair usually, although I used to get highlights every other month that kept my hair a light, shiny brown. But once I realized Mom couldn't stop me anymore, I let it grow out dark, so with the hair dye it ends up being this kind of a dark forest green. You can't spot the green right away in most lights, but in the sunshine suddenly you're like, *Poof, emerald!*

Well, *I* think it's cool.

My mom would have had a heart attack. We used to have enormous fights because I wanted a belly button ring (which I now have, thanks very much). Olympia just wrinkled her nose at my dark green hair, then shrugged and said, "I've seen worse."

That pretty much sums up the difference in their parenting styles.

After breakfast, Crystal carefully applied eyeliner and mascara and lipstick to my face. I had to be very stern with her when she pulled out the bright green eye shadow, though. She loves bright colors (I know, it's not very vampire-y of her) and she insisted it would look perfect with my eyes. Crystal has told me a few times that my eyes are greener than they used to be, in sort of an iridescent way. I'd really like to check this out myself, but of course that's impossible. However, I can still be pretty sure that bright green eye shadow is not the way to go.

"Oh, fine," Crystal huffed. "I suppose you look very pretty anyway."

She helped me pick out a jean miniskirt, knee-high black boots and black tights, and a green fitted tee with a grumpy-looking anime panda on it. I added a black hoodie, since it was early October and starting to get colder outside. You know how vampires in the old movies wore big cloaks with the collars turned up, all sinister-like? Wilhelm says he used to wear those all the time, because it was a great way to hide your face if a mirror popped up. Hooded sweatshirts are the same way, like the modern-day version of those cloaks, stylish and updated for hip teenage vampires of the twenty-first century.

"*So* cute," Crystal proclaimed.

"Really?" I said, turning around and trying to figure out what I looked like. "So cute that you'd spill your deepest, darkest secrets to me? Like, for instance, that you threw a guy out a window a couple days ago?"

Crystal tilted her head the other way. "Maybe not *that* cute," she said.

"Oh, thanks."

"But if you had some green eye shadow—" she added hopefully.

"Come *on*, Kira!" Zach yelled from downstairs as I ducked away from Crystal and grabbed my book bag. "We don't want to miss the big mourning assembly!"

Oh, man. The school had had one of these assemblies on the first day, so that everyone could get together and grieve about some ancient French teacher who'd died over the summer. It was wicked boring when you didn't know the person being mourned. On the other hand, if my Ann Arbor school had had one of these for me, that'd be okay. I'd have to ask Olympia if they did; she was the one who filled me in about my funeral and everything, which I missed, what with how busy I was being really dead and all. It takes a couple days of being a corpse before a vampire rises.

Zach and I were early to school, as usual, so I lurked around the gym doors while everyone else filed in and found seats on the bleachers. I was watching for any of my suspects. I knew I should start by talking to Rowan—you couldn't get more suspicious than what he'd said to his dad yesterday—but part of me was hoping that smiley guy would walk in first. Or, you know,

Daniel . . . that'd be okay, too.

I poked around inside my book bag as if I was looking for something while everyone went by. It was a lot quieter than our normal assemblies; I heard a few muffled sobs and a lot of shocked and curious whispering. The football team is usually the noisiest group, pounding on bleachers as they go by and whooping to each other across the gym. But today they were subdued, shuffling along with their heads down. I'm no fan of jocks, but even I felt sorry, seeing them like that. Tex had been a doofus, but from everything I'd heard about him, he'd been a well-liked, good-natured doofus. Not the kind of obnoxious guy with lots of enemies who usually gets murdered, at least on TV.

A few minutes before the bell rang, I finally spotted Rowan's big combat boots stomping through the doors. The hood of his black sweatshirt was up and his shoulders were hunched. He didn't look at anyone as he slouched into the gym and climbed the bleachers, taking two at a time with his long, skinny legs. He reached the top and sat down, way back from the gym floor—far from most of the football players and cheerleaders, who were sitting in the front two rows, sniffling and consoling each other.

I already knew that my one new friend in town, Vivi, wasn't coming to the assembly. She'd emailed me last night that she was "too overcome" and "shattered" by the whole murder thing (even though I was pretty sure she didn't really know Tex). Her parents were letting her stay home for the rest of the week. There was no sign of Daniel or Smiley Guy either. So I took a deep breath, scrambled up the bleachers, and casually plunked myself down next to Rowan.

"Mind if I sit here?" I asked.

His long red-brown bangs hung over his face as he leaned his elbows on his knees. He pushed his hood back a little to give me a nod. I saw him notice my legs first, and then his gaze traveled up to my face.

Now, I'm not drop-dead gorgeous like Vivi is, but I think—given my tasteful emerald nose stud and my half-Japanese features and my striking, dark green hair—that I'm not exactly the most horrifying teenage girl on the face of the planet.

But when Rowan met my eyes, he gave me a look that said exactly that. In fact, he looked so spooked that for a moment I thought he was either going to scream and dive off the bleachers or have a heart attack and literally die right there in front of me. Which would make it much harder to get him to confess to a murder, don't you think?

"Who . . . what . . . ?" he stammered. He actually started to get to his feet like he was going to run away.

"Whoa, what's wrong?" I asked, touching his shoulder. "Are you okay?" I've found, in my limited experience, that touching a guy lightly in a nonthreatening, quasi-flirty manner is a good way to get him to stay put. It totally worked this time, too. Then again, the principal was tapping his microphone at that same moment, so possibly Rowan just wanted to avoid making a scene. But let's assume it was me.

He sat down again, putting one hand on his narrow chest and taking a couple of deep breaths. Maybe he was just startled to find a girl talking to him. He seemed like someone who kept to himself; hot girls probably didn't talk to him very often. Or even semi-cute girls like me. Maybe that was what had scared him.

His skin was really pale, even paler than Vivi's, and she's a natural redhead who looks as though she's made of porcelain. Rowan's eyes were an interesting dark blue, like the evening sky just before the stars come out. If I dyed my hair blue instead of green, it'd probably end up being that color. And his eyelashes were really startlingly long. I kind of wanted to touch them to see if they were real, but of course I didn't do that. He stared at me for a long moment, his eyes flicking from my hair to my multiple earrings to my shimmery green nail polish.

"Do I know you?" he finally asked in his soft, mossy voice.

That surprised me. "I don't think so," I said. *Uh-oh.* Maybe his vampire radar was a lot better than mine. Could he tell there was something inhuman about me? Was he afraid I was here to expose him? Or what if we'd attended the same summer camp as kids or something? I didn't recognize him, but he might have known me when I was Phoebe Tanaka.

Quickly I said, "I'm Kira. Kira November." We pick new names as vampires, obviously, or else someone from our past would be liable to find us someday while surfing the Internet or something. Zach, for instance, used to be Cash. We were stuck with the last name November (Olympia's choice several decades ago), but I chose Kira.

"Kira," Rowan echoed, looking confused. "You look familiar."

"You've probably seen me around school," I said. "Or maybe it's 'cause I look like the actress from *Samurai Girl*. I get that a lot." Sure, in wishful-thinking world. But I didn't want him to connect the dots if he did sense my vampireness.

"I don't—" he began, but then the principal started to speak, and I went, "Shhhh," hoping he'd forget all about it by the time the assembly was over.

Principal Lovato went on for a long time about what a stand-up guy Tex was and what a treasure he was to the school and how much everyone liked him and how his smile lit up the halls. It actually sounded like he knew who he was talking about, instead of making up stuff about some student he couldn't remember. I guess being star quarterback nets you some decent eulogies. Several cheerleaders in the front row were sobbing, their mascara streaking their faces.

I snuck a notebook out of my bag, opened it to a blank page, and scribbled, *Did you know Tex?* at the top, then handed it to Rowan.

He looked at my notebook for a long moment, like it was a spider that had just landed in his lap. But finally he took my pen and wrote, *No.*

All right, Mr. Chatty.

I took the pen back, letting my fingers lightly brush his, and wrote, *Me neither. We just moved here a month ago from Florida.* Olympia makes up backstories for us (and produces supporting documents like magic) every time we move. Usually they're not too far off from our real story, so they're easier to remember.

After another long pause, he took the pen again and wrote, *Same. Two years ago. From California.*

California! I wrote. I'd never been there. So there's no way he could've known Phoebe-me. *Cool. What part?*

Excruciatingly long pause. *San Francisco.*

Oh, I wrote. *Hilly. Right?*

This time he just shrugged.

Well. This was going swimmingly. I could tell that deep, dark secrets were going to come pouring out of him any second.

I realized that he hadn't introduced himself yet. *What's your name?* I wrote. He couldn't answer *that* with a shrug.

Rowan.

All right. Now I knew almost exactly as much as I had when I'd sat down. Maybe it was time to try a more direct approach.

Poor Tex, I tried. *I was so shocked when we got to school yesterday. Did you see the body?*

He touched the page with his long fingers, staring at my handwriting. After a moment, I nudged the pen into his hand and he wrote, *What body?*

Um. Okaaaaaay.

Tex's body, I wrote.

No, he wrote quickly. *Yes. Not really.*

82

Pause. I wrestled the pen away from him.

Lots of blood, huh? I watched his face closely as he read that, checking for an expression that might say, "Yeah, ew," or "Mmm, hungry" or "Yeeessss, *I* did that."

But his expression told me nothing quite that clear. He just gazed at the page like he was looking right through it.

I'd never seen a dead body before, I tried.

Almost immediately he seized the pen from my fingers and scribbled, *I wrote a poem about it.*

So he really *was* Poet Guy. Look at me, all insightful. I'd have this case cracked in no time.

Can I see your poem? I wrote.

Not yet. Not finished.

What's it called?

In spiky capital letters, he wrote one word: *BLOOD.*

Chapter 7

Well, my job here is done, I thought. I was about ready to grab his wrist and confirm that he had no pulse, when the assembly suddenly ended. Rowan bolted to his feet right away, but he couldn't get out without stepping on a lot of other people, so he was stuck there for a moment.

"Awesome to meet you, Rowan," I said, standing up and putting away my notebook. I tried to look cute and flirty and not at all creeped out. "Maybe we can eat lunch together sometime."

Now I finally got my first real boy reaction from him: He blushed and shoved his hands in his pockets awkwardly.

"Really?" he said. "You wanna eat with me?"

"Sure," I said. "Maybe you can show me your poetry or something."

"Yeah, all right," he said. "If you really want

to see it. It's not very good. My photography is better."

"Oh, I love photography," I said, giving him my most winning smile.

You know how in movies (at least, in Jake Gyllenhaal movies, which are all I would watch if I had a choice) there's always that moment when you see the hero gazing at the heroine with this intense, yearning, deeply meaningful look in his eyes?

In real life it kind of knocks your socks off. I completely forgot that there were students clomping and thumping on the bleachers all around us. It was like Rowan and I were the only real, three-dimensional things against a flat background. He must have felt it, too, because his awkwardness seemed to melt away. He reached out and trailed his fingers lightly down my cheek to my chin.

"Maybe I could photograph you," he said softly.

Was I being mesmerized? Was he pulling vampire tricks on me? Was it even possible for a vampire to mesmerize another vampire? I had no idea. Perhaps he was just a strangely compelling, regular guy with really cool eyes. Maybe I hadn't eaten enough for breakfast, and that's why I was feeling light-headed. . . .

Someone jumped down the bleachers and jostled into Rowan, and he dropped his hand quickly. "See you," he mumbled, ducking his head. Hunching his shoulders again, he hurried away into the crowd.

Well.

Solving this mystery wasn't such a bad assignment after all. Apart from the fact that one of these totally cute boys was also a murderer, of course. Rowan's clue sheet might say "Cool eyes" and "Potentially sensitive soul" but it also had to say "Poetry about blood . . . creepy? YES."

I was still in a daze when I got to my history classroom, but everyone was freaked out by the assembly, so Mr. Wright just gave us a chapter to read and then sat at the front of the room watching us faux-sympathetically with a phony *Talk to me if you need to* expression.

And then, five minutes later, Daniel walked in.

He was even better-looking in the light, although today he was wearing a long-sleeved dove-gray shirt that hid his abs, which I didn't approve of. He handed a note to the teacher, scanned the classroom, and spotted me. He smiled in that slow, charming way and gave me a wink. I saw a couple of the cheerleaders twist around to check who he was winking at. Apparently mourning for Tex wasn't going to stop them from keeping an eye on the new hot boy and any potential gossip.

I was sitting in the back row, mainly because it was out of the path of the sunlight coming through the windows. It so happened that there was an empty desk next to mine. If he sat there, would it be because of me? Or would he just be avoiding the sun, too?

"Class," the teacher said, "let me introduce our new student, Daniel Marvel. It's a tough day to be starting out here, so I hope you'll all be welcoming to him."

Yes, please, I thought. *I'd like to be very welcoming to him.*

"It's so odd," said Mr. Wright, handing the slip of paper back to Daniel. "Normally we have a little warning about new students. I had no idea you were coming."

Daniel shrugged. "That's what the principal said," he said innocently, "but my parents cleared my transfer to the school a month ago."

Oh, did they? I wondered. *Or did someone, ahem, sneak into the school last night and put you in there?* Was that really why he'd been here in the middle of the night? But if he'd killed Tex, why would he be sticking around afterward? Surely most vampires don't have to keep going to high school once they're, you know, like, a hundred years old. I don't care if I still look sixteen; one diploma is all I intend to get.

"Huh," said Mr. Wright. "All right, take a seat."

Daniel sauntered down the aisle and slipped right into that seat beside me. Blond heads in the front row swiveled and craned to get a look at him. Did I mention how hot he is?

"Hey, there," he said to me.

"Hey, there yourself," I said. "You missed the assembly this morning."

"Forms," he said, spreading his hands. "There seemed to be an awful lot of them. I think a certain guidance counselor didn't want my first experience of the school to involve funeral services."

"Count yourself lucky," I said. "It was long and tragic. Can I see your schedule?"

"Shhh," said Mr. Wright, but sort of half-heartedly.

Daniel slid a piece of paper out of his note-book and passed it to me. All of his movements were graceful, like those of a cat or a panther or a really well-trained dancer.

I ran my eyes down his schedule.

He was in every single one of my classes.

I shot a glance at him. He had his eyes on his history book, leaning back calmly in his chair as if this were the most natural place in the world for him to be.

Was it a coincidence? Or had he done that on purpose? Maybe I was reading too much into it. At least one of the cheerleaders and a couple of band guys from the woodwinds section were in all my classes, too. Surely that happened all the time.

And Daniel couldn't have changed his sched-ule last night *after* meeting me, because we'd left the school together.

Right?

We kept quiet for the rest of class, but when

the bell rang, I leaned over and said, "Want to hear something freaky? We have the exact same schedule."

He gave me that wry little smile. "That sounds very fortuitous. Does that mean you can lead me to"—he glanced down at his schedule—"physics?"

"Sadly for you, yes," I said. We gathered our books as I told him about our scatterbrained physics teacher. When we walked down the hall together, he stayed close beside me, and a few times his arm brushed mine as we swerved around the rampaging hordes.

It felt so normal, you could almost forget the whole meeting-in-a-dark-hall-at-a-murder-scene thing.

Speaking of which, I still had one suspect to check off my dance card, and I didn't even know his name yet. Part of me thought, *Aren't* two *dreamy, mysterious guys enough for you to investigate?* But I couldn't shake the feeling that I needed to know more about the guy with the cute smile. Not because of the cute smile, mind you. No, no, no. I was interested in the way he'd looked at the murder scene. Surely that warranted further investigation.

And then finally, at the end of the day, I saw him.

I had just left Daniel at his locker, which was on the first floor because all the regular junior lockers on the top floor were taken. I was on my way toward the school's back exit, hoping that if I snuck out that way and headed through the cemetery, I'd make it home before Zach did. He was always trying to walk home with me, but I usually managed to give him the slip.

Between the main body of the school and the cafeteria and gym buildings, there's a little court-yard with benches and trees and tables where the upperclassmen usually eat lunch. Luckily for me, Vivi prefers to eat inside because of her delicate, easily sunburned skin—yet another reason I'm friends with her.

I happened to glance out there as I went by, and there he was: Mr. Smiley, sitting on one of the tables and joking around with a couple of muscular blond guys.

I stopped by the door to the courtyard and

reapplied my lip gloss, watching him surreptitiously. This was a bad sign—or a good sign, I suppose, depending on whether I wanted him to turn out to be a murdering vampire or not. He was sitting right out in the sunshine, which seemed like a very un-vampire-y thing to do, unless his supercharged vampire sunscreen was a lot more powerful than mine. His sunglasses were pushed up on his head, holding back his curly mop of dark hair, and I could see gold flecks in his brown eyes. The sleeves of his faded blue shirt were rolled up, revealing toned arms.

How was I going to meet him? I could just saunter out there and say hi, but (a) sunshine, and (b) would that make him suspicious? Like, *Why is a random girl talking to me? Oh, and also, gee, the sunlight sure seems to make her dizzy. . . . Hmmmm.*

What I really wanted was some way for us to "meet cute"—you know, like in a movie, where the hero and heroine accidentally run into each other and it's hilarious, and then of course they fall in love. Except, of course, we'd skip the "falling in love" part if it turned out that Mr.

Smiley liked to savagely bite people and throw them out of windows.

I listened with my vampire hearing, hoping that something would give me an idea.

"All right, I'm heading home," said one of the blond guys. "Need a lift?"

"Sure," said the other blond guy.

"Nah. Thanks, though. I brought my car today," said my guy. He had an accent! A cute accent, kind of British-sounding—maybe Australian or South African. "I think I'll do a few more laps before I go."

Laps? Like around the track? That wasn't going to help me. There was even *more* sunshine out there.

"You're a machine," the first blond guy laughed. "My arms are way too sore after this morning."

Arms? Who ran around the track on their arms?

"Yeah, but that's 'cause you're a wuss," my guy said kindly. He cracked up as the first guy pushed him off the table.

"One day I'm going to put ants in your swimsuit, and then you'll finally lose a meet," the second blond guy teased.

Aha.

They were on the swim team!

Something poked at my memory. Tex had mentioned the swim team in his last blog post. Something about how he'd quit swimming—which meant these guys probably knew him. Now I had even more reason to meet Mr. Smiley.

And I knew just how to do it.

Chapter 8

I'd heard that Luna High had an indoor pool somewhere (an outdoor pool in Massachusetts wouldn't be the most useful thing), but I hadn't seen it yet. My plan was only going to work if there were no mirrors there and nobody else was around, so I had to get there before Mr. Smiley did.

I left him as he said goodbye to his friends, and I hurried down the long hallway to the gym, passing the boys' and girls' locker rooms. Luna High is much too big, if you ask me, but Olympia likes to live in places where we fade into the crowd. The gym is enormous, with a fitness center and a climbing wall and tennis courts and all kinds of nonsense that would have just added to my suffering when I was a regular teenager. Having vampire strength does make P.E. a lot more bearable.

Apparently most of the after-school sports today had been canceled in honor of Tex. There were a few students in the gym, but nobody paid any attention to me as I slipped by and headed down the stairs to the pool area. Big windows overlooked the pool from the gym, but it seemed unlikely that anyone would be looking down at it today. A sign on the door said that regular pool hours were canceled as well.

I was relieved to find the pool deserted. Perfect turquoise-blue water stretched out in front of me, divided into six lanes. Clean white equipment was stacked around the pool, and the bleachers waited blankly. It was very quiet, with only a few noises filtering down from the cars and people outside.

No mirrors, and the only windows were high in the ceiling, so the room was bright but no direct sunshine hit the pool or the ground around it. A perfect place for athletic vampires. *I should tell Zach about this*, I thought. He missed being a high school jock, and most sports were kind of out due to the high sunshine factor. Maybe he could join the swim team. *If he ever stops being a jerk, I'll mention it.*

Two doors on either side of the stairwell led to the changing rooms. I dropped my book bag by the stairs and pressed my ear to the door that said BOYS.

After a while, I heard footsteps inside. As I'd hoped, Mr. Smiley had gone through the boys' locker room . . . assuming it was him. I really *hoped* it was him. I didn't want to waste this extremely cute meeting on some random guy.

Somewhere inside, a locker slammed. He'd be coming out soon.

I hurried over to the pool, finger-combing my hair. Alas, my poor outfit. This had better be worth it. I started walking along the edge of the pool, glancing down at the clear blue water. I could see straight down to the gleaming white tiles at the bottom.

The changing room door creaked open behind me.

"Oh, excuse me—hello?" It was exactly the cute accent I'd been waiting for.

I whirled around with a little yelp of surprise, saw him standing in the doorway, and promptly toppled into the pool.

It was *much colder* than I'd expected. I completely forgot about the guy for a minute as my entire body shrieked, "OH, MY GOD! FREEZING!" I flailed my arms and went under as water flooded up my nose. Vampires can't drown—we don't even need to breathe, although most of us still do, instinctively. But we can still, apparently, get water up our noses. Somehow this was not as romantic as I'd been hoping.

Until suddenly . . . there was another splash, and then a pair of strong brown arms wrapped around me. I felt myself pressed to his warm, bare chest as he kicked up to the surface. I put my arms around his neck and held on, my face *thisclose* to the curve of his collarbone.

We bobbed to the surface next to the wall. He kept one arm around my waist and grabbed the wall with his other hand. Reluctantly, I let go with one hand and did the same. Now we were facing each other, hanging on to the wall with our other arms still around each other. His lips were only a few inches from mine, and now he was giving me the adorable smile I'd had in my head since yesterday.

Apart from the fact that I was now freezing and my clothes were all wet, this was exactly what I'd been hoping for.

"Are you all right?" he asked.

I nodded. "J-j-just b-b-b-brrrrr—" Okay, maybe the teeth chattering wasn't precisely part of the plan.

"There's a ladder over here," he said, taking my hand and towing me a few feet down the wall. He guided me onto the rungs and I climbed out, shivering. He hopped out right behind me and ran over to a stack of red and gold towels by the wall. Grabbing a few of them, he ran back to me. I was trying to smooth my wet hair back into something presentable when he came up behind me and wrapped a towel around my shoulders. Somehow *he* still felt warm. I wished he'd keep his arms around me, but he moved his hands to my arms and rubbed them through the towel . . . which was okay, too.

"You'll feel better in a minute," he said. "That was absolutely spectacular."

"Oh, good," I said, returning his smile. "Spectacular is what I was going for." He guided me over to a bench and we sat down, but he kept rubbing my arms. It was, frankly, the nicest feeling I'd had since the early days with Zach.

"Yeah, I'd give you a nine-point-five," he said. "I have to deduct half a point for missing the diving board completely, of course."

"Well, I owe it all to my great coach," I said with a pointed look. "His method involves scaring the living daylights out of me."

"Sorry," he said, looking guilty. "I didn't think there'd be anyone else in here. You're not supposed to swim without a lifeguard, you know."

"I wasn't *going* to swim," I said. "That was most definitely *not* on my agenda." I waved a hand at my sad, dripping clothes. "You look like *you* were about to break that rule, though."

He was wearing dark red swimming trunks and nothing else. This was definitely a good way to meet him . . . and his arms . . . and his shoulders . . . and his pecs. . . .

"Busted," he said, toweling off his hair with a sheepish grin. "I figured a few laps wouldn't hurt, even though the regular lifeguard wouldn't be here. On a day like today, the coaches have bigger things to worry about."

"I'm Kira," I said.

"Milo," he said, offering me his hand. He wasn't very tall—only a few inches taller than me—but his hands were surprisingly big and very strong. *Milo*, I thought as his fingers wrapped around mine. *Finally a name to go with the smile.*

"Are you new here?" he asked.

"Yeah," I said. "We just moved up from Florida this summer. I figured I'd check out the pool while there was no one around, but I didn't intend to give it quite such a close inspection."

He grinned. "Well, next time remember to wear your water wings."

"Hey!" I said indignantly. "I'll have you know I'm actually a very good swimmer."

"Oh, clearly," he teased.

"Hello, boots!" I said, pointing to them. "Also, I was startled!" He started laughing and I smacked his shoulder. "You should be begging my forgiveness, not making fun of me."

"I do beg your forgiveness," Milo said. "How will you *ever* forgive me?"

"Well, the heroic rescue helped," I said,

pulling off my boots and pouring the water out of them. "If there's any way you can get me dry so I can head home, that'd give you some brownie points, too."

"I have an extra shirt in my locker," Milo said. "I wore it yesterday, though—do you mind?"

"Not if it's drier than this one," I said, lifting the bottom of my shirt and squeezing it out. Rivulets of water streamed to the ground. I totally spotted him noticing my belly button ring. "I can probably squeak home in these," I said, nudging my boots. "It's only a twenty-minute walk," I added with a forlorn sigh.

"No way!" Milo said, just as I'd hoped. "Let me drive you. I have a car."

"You have a car?" I said, pretending to swoon. "*And* a dry shirt? Where have you been hiding all my life?"

He laughed. "Probably in the pool. Let's get my shirt. There's no one in the guys' changing room, don't worry." He stood up and offered me his hand. I took it, feeling warm and fuzzy, and not just from the fluffy towel wrapped around my shoulders. We walked down the length of the pool to the changing room doors. I wondered if he could feel my smile radiating throughout my whole body. This was silly. I'd only just met the guy. And I had Daniel and Rowan to think about. So why did I think Milo was so very cute? Just because he made me laugh?

As we pushed through the door into the changing room, something made me glance back at the windows overlooking the pool, and a shiver ran down my spine.

I couldn't be sure—but for a moment I thought I caught a glimpse of someone standing up in the windows, watching the pool.

Watching *us*.

Chapter 9

The door swung shut behind us before I could tell who had been standing above the pool, or even if I'd really seen what I thought I had. If I was right, it was someone tall—a guy, I was pretty sure. I hoped it wasn't Zach stalking me around school again. On the other hand, at least I was used to that. . . . Someone else stalking me would be way more creepy.

"Welcome to our secret lair," Milo said with a grin, waving at the green-tiled walls around us. "I promise not to tell anyone you were in here if you promise not to reveal our nefarious secrets."

"Such as the fact that your changing room looks exactly like ours?" I joked. "Except our lockers are yellow." The lockers in here were red. I could see the door at the other end, leading to the main guys' locker room. I did an instinctive check—no mirrors. There was a mirror in the girls' changing room, but apparently boys didn't need to check their bathing suits obsessively the way we did. At least, whoever had built the place thought so.

Milo spun the combination on his locker and pulled out a pale orange T-shirt. It was as soft as a teddy bear and it smelled like him— cinnamon and sunshine and tangerines and clean laundry.

"There are these, too, if you're not too horri- fied to wear them," he said, pulling out a pair of giant red flip-flops bearing the school's LHS logo in gold.

"I think being able to walk is worth a little fashion crisis," I said.

Milo chivalrously turned around and cov- ered his eyes while I wiggled out of my wet tights and shirt. The flip-flops were enormous on my feet, but better than going barefoot. The shirt was also really big on me, but cozy and comfortable.

"Okay," I said when it was safe for him to turn around again. He hid a smile and I wrinkled my nose at him. "You can't laugh at me; these are *your* clothes."

"That shirt looks much better on you than it does on me," he said gallantly (and, I'm sure, inaccurately). He reached to brush my hair back off my shoulder and then stopped. He picked up a lock of my hair and squinted at it. "Is your hair green?"

"No!" I said, sounding shocked. "Wow, the chlorine in your pool must be really strong!"

He looked so worried, I nearly fell over laughing.

"You goof," he said, poking my arm. "I've never met anyone with green hair before."

I shrugged. "I figured, new school, new me." I gathered my wet clothes and boots into a plastic bag while Milo got dressed.

"I know what you mean," he said. "Last time I moved was when I decided to go out for swimming. Before that I was really into playing the guitar, and before that, tae kwon do." We headed for the exit, back through the pool room.

"Wow, really?" I said. "And you just left those

behind each time you moved?" *Is that a vampire thing? I could do that, too . . . at the next school, try out for the school play . . . at the one after that, become an ice skater. . . . I could try out a whole bunch of different lives and see which one I like best. Although, if it means reliving high school over and over again, then never mind.*

"Don't worry," he said. "I kept the really important things, like my comic book collection." He winced and slapped his forehead. "Now *that's* on the top ten things not to tell a cute girl when you first meet her, isn't it?"

I beamed. "You can if you tell her she's cute at the same time."

He looked like he couldn't stop smiling any more than I could. I grabbed my book bag as we went up the stairs and out through the empty gym into the parking lot. If someone really had been watching us earlier, he was gone now.

Milo's car was this tiny, beat-up black thing with stuff scattered all over the seats. In the backseat I spied crumpled papers and several science fiction books, including one with a pair of fangs on the cover. Research on his own kind, or just one of the recent wave of vampire novels?

Milo dove into the passenger seat and started tossing things into the back. I noticed there weren't any food wrappers, which was nice—Zach's car used to be full of crumpled McDonald's bags. Milo just had a lot of water bottles, most of them half full. He flung a pair of goggles and a beach towel in the back and stood aside.

"Sorry about the mess," he said ruefully.

"That's okay," I said. "Maybe I should sit on that towel, actually—my skirt's still pretty wet."

"What care I for upholstery," he declared, "when milady is beside me?"

I giggled. "All right, I'll get it." I leaned over the seat and grabbed the towel, giving Milo a very intentional view of my legs as I did. I hoped it wasn't my imagination that he looked a little more bedazzled when I turned around.

He closed the door gently behind me and hurried around to the driver's side. I told him my address as he started the car.

"Ooo, the spooky part of town," he said.

"There's a spooky part?" I said.

"What's more important, there's a non-spooky part," he said. "Can I buy you an ice cream before I take you home? I feel like it's the least I can do after scaring your shirt off." He paused. "That came out wrong."

"I will never say no to ice cream," I said with a grin. "If you really don't mind being seen with me like this."

"Not at all," he said. "Hang on a minute." He leaned into the back and grabbed a notebook and pen. Turning to a blank page, he put on a studious look and wrote, murmuring: *Never says no to ice cream.*

"Oh, we're taking notes on me now?" I said, laughing. "Here, let me help." I took the pen and notebook out of his hand and added *Likes very expensive jewelry* to the list as he pulled out of the parking lot.

"Let me guess," he said. "Jade and emerald especially?"

"Oh, no, am I totally predictable?" I said.

"Hardly," he said. "I can just tell that green is your color."

"What tipped you off?" I asked. "The toenail polish?"

He gave my feet that cute smile. "Man, it's nice to hang out with someone who isn't all doom and gloom today," he said.

I stopped smiling. "I'm sorry—I didn't even think. Were you friends with Tex?"

"Not really." He shook his head. "We played basketball together sometimes, and we were on the swim team together last year, but he quit this year. He said he wanted to focus on football, which is kind of dumb since the seasons don't overlap, but it didn't bother the rest of us. Not to speak disrespectfully of the dead, but Tex wasn't the greatest swimmer." He whispered the last part, then glanced over at me. "All my friends have been moping around all day. . . . I just want to forget about it for a while."

"Okay," I said. "It's such a freaky thing. I'd never seen a dead body before."

"I have," Milo said, and for the first time I heard something serious and steely in his voice. He glanced at me again. "Sorry, I don't want to freak you out. Really, this is a great town. You'll love it here. Please don't ever leave." He grinned.

"You saw another dead body *here*?" I said.

He made a face. "A couple years ago. It was my welcome to a new town, too—I guess we have that in common."

"Was it also a murder?" I asked.

"Everyone thinks so," he said. "But it was never solved. The victim was just a random guy in a dark alley. Whoever did it didn't even take his wallet."

I wanted to know if that was a vampire attack, too, but how exactly would I ask that? *Notice any bite marks?* Yeah, I didn't think so.

"I'm making a great impression, aren't I?" Milo said. "Don't think about it. I'm sure all small towns have mysterious murders hidden in their pasts. Think about me instead! Doesn't my presence make up for a little blood and gore?"

"I guess it does," I said, "if there's really ice cream at the end of this trip. But it sounds like you move a lot. How do I know you're going to stick around?"

"We'll be here for a while, I think," Milo said.

"My dad's involved in this never-ending proj-ect." *Literally never-ending?* I wondered. *Like, in a vampire way?* "Why did you guys move here?" he asked.

"The weather," I said.

He shot me a look. "You've *got* to be kidding. Do you know what Massachusetts winters are like?"

"My mom missed the seasons," I said, lift-ing my shoulders. "My parents both work from home, so we can live wherever." But I really didn't want to talk about *my* family. "Do you have any brothers or sisters?"

"No, it's just me and my dad," he said. "You?"

Yeah, that change of subject went well. "My older sister, Crystal, and her husband live with us," I said. It's funny how easy the lies were now; in Georgia I nearly messed up a hundred times. "And my brother, Zach, is a year older than me." Well, sort of.

"Zach," Milo said, his brow furrowing. "I met a new guy named Zach last week in P.E., but he doesn't look anything like you."

"Yeah, he doesn't, luckily for me," I said. "I'm adopted." To put it mildly.

"Wow," said Milo. "Do you know anything about your birth parents? Is that a rude question?"

"It's okay," I said. "I don't." That was certainly the easiest answer.

"Oh," he said, turning into a small parking lot. There was a barn at one end with a counter sticking out of it, and tables were arranged under a shady overhang. Only one other couple was there, a pair of senior citizens sharing a cup of chocolate ice cream with rainbow sprinkles. They looked sweet together.

Milo noticed the direction of my gaze. "Maybe that'll be us in eighty years," he said. So cute.

That'll never be me, I realized. *I'm never going to grow old with someone. People will look at me and always see an obnoxious teenager.*

"Wow, it's nice to know this date is going somewhere," I joked.

He blushed.

Uh-oh. Did I just say "date"?

"You're not like other girls," he observed, turning off the car.

That is . . . really true.

"Sure, I am," I said, batting my eyelashes at him. "For instance, I really, seriously love ice cream."

Although, to be fair, I can eat a lot more ice cream than other girls can. Milo's eyebrows went up when he saw the triple-scoop chocolate, banana, and peanut butter ice cream I ordered. With chocolate sprinkles on top, of course.

"Don't be alarmed," I said with a wicked smile. "My metabolism can handle it."

"I'm not alarmed, I'm impressed," he said. His solitary scoop of blackberry chocolate chip looked lonely next to my cup. I scooped some sprinkles onto his dish, and he stole some of my peanut butter ice cream, laughing when I fended him off with my spoon.

I couldn't believe I was on a date. A real date, with a boy much funnier and smarter and cuter than Zach, and therefore the best date I'd had since dying. I didn't care if my investigation went nowhere right now. Maybe I'd only imagined the look Milo had given Tex's body. I figured I could investigate Rowan and Daniel later; at that moment it was fine with me if Milo had nothing to do with blood and corpses. I mean, maybe it would be convenient for me if he happened to be a vampire, too, but I'd rather not find out if he had a predilection for eating football players.

Just as I was thinking that, he leaned forward to steal some more of my ice cream, and under his shirt collar I saw the necklace that I had spotted yesterday. The black leather rope held a small silver pendant with an unfamiliar symbol carved on it. But that wasn't all.

There were red beads knotted into the necklace . . . and one of them was missing.

Chapter 10

After Milo dropped me off at home, I hung up my wet clothes and dug my jeans out of the pile at the bottom of my bed. In the left pocket was the red bead I'd found at the murder scene. I examined it in the low light from my bedside lamp. It was a deep, rich scarlet, the color of a drop of blood. And it looked exactly like the ones in Milo's necklace.

What does that mean?

Well, for one thing, it meant I was right to think I should investigate him. So . . . yay, me?

Of course, there could be a normal explanation. He could easily have lost it there sometime during the day before the murder.

Or . . . he could have lost it during the struggle if, say, he *was* the murderer.

But he seemed so . . . non-murder-y. He was

all ice cream and puppies and sexy swimmer's arms. Why would he kill Tex?

Why would anyone?

Was this just a hungry vampire attack? Or did someone have a good reason for killing the school's star quarterback?

Maybe I needed to find out more about Tex.

I fell asleep thinking about this, trying to make my sun headache go away. I dreamed that Milo and I were swimming together, up and down the length of the pool. I beat him to the wall, but when I turned around, Milo was gone and Daniel was floating faceup beside me.

"Where's Milo?" I asked.

He pointed, and I looked up to the windows where Rowan was standing, looking down at us in the pool.

"That's Rowan," I said.

"Is it?" said Daniel, and then I looked down and realized the pool water had turned to blood.

I woke up feeling muddled and sticky. It was late at night but not yet midnight. I needed some moonlight to clear my head.

Bert and Crystal were curled up on the couch in the den, watching a black-and-white horror movie on TV. Zach was sitting at the kitchen counter with a peanut butter-and-blood sandwich on a plate beside him. His calculus book was open and his notebook was out, but he was just staring at the pages blankly.

"That looks like it's going well," I said, grabbing a soda from the fridge.

"I hate this stuff," he said. "We're getting a take-home exam to do over the weekend, and I just know I'm going to fail. It sucks so much—when I was a basketball star, the cheerleaders did my math homework for me."

"Really?" I said. "Cheerleaders?"

"I didn't say they did it *right*," he said with a lopsided grin. Aww, Zach being funny without being slimy. I hadn't seen that in a while.

I laughed. "Wish I could help," I said, "but I can barely handle pre-calculus. Those squiggly things of yours are making me nervous from all the way over here."

"Too bad," he said, leering. "Doing homework together can be pretty romantic."

I stuck out my tongue at him and went to find Olympia.

"I don't think she's up yet," Crystal called

when I rapped on the door of Olympia's office.

I knocked as I opened the door to the basement—although if they were asleep, I knew they wouldn't be able to hear me. Wilhelm and Olympia give new meaning to "sleep like the dead." The wooden stairs creaked under my sneakers as I headed down into the dark. I fumbled over my head as I reached the bottom step and tugged on the pull chain, turning on the solitary lightbulb. It barely lit up the damp concrete corners of the room, stuffed with old furniture and piles of boxes. Olympia had bought most of it just to fill up the space. The hope was that if anyone came down here, they'd be too overwhelmed and discouraged by the amount of worthless old stuff to actually poke around and notice anything.

I wove between two faded russet armchairs and climbed over an upside-down paisley purple couch. In the back corner, where it was most shadowy, I opened a big mahogany wardrobe and tapped on the back wall.

After a moment, the "wall" slid back and I jumped down into Wilhelm and Olympia's crypt. I mean, it's just a room, but it's decorated like a crypt and it feels like a crypt, so that's what I call it. Two fat black candles flickered gloomily on a low table between the two coffins. I know, I keep telling them it's really cliché, but that gets Wilhelm all hot and bothered, and then he yells at me about tradition and respect and whatever. Do what you like, but you're not going to catch *me* sleeping in a place like this.

The walls and floor are gray concrete, but a thick red rug is spread across the floor, so I left my shoes at the entrance before tiptoeing over to Olympia's coffin. The lid was open, and she was lying faceup with her hands folded over her chest, perfectly still. Her long jet-black hair was spread out in a fan over the white silk lining.

"Olympia," I whispered.

She opened one eye and peered at me.

"Oh. Kira," she said. "No need to whisper. He's awake."

I turned and looked at Wilhelm's coffin, but it was empty. "Oh," I said. "I didn't see him upstairs."

"That's because he's right there," Olympia said, nodding at a corner of the ceiling. I squinted and saw a tiny, leathery brown bat hanging upside down. I used to think bats were spooky, until I acquired a dad who turns into one all the time.

"When do I get to do that?" I asked.

"Most vampires take about three hundred years to evolve that skill," Olympia said. "Wilhelm is one of the rare few who could do it from the beginning. Some vampires are like that."

"So there might be some other neat power I can do already, even though I'm not supposed to yet?" I asked. "Like, say . . . flying?"

"I think we'd have noticed if you could fly," Olympia said dryly. "Can I help you with something?"

"You're on good terms with the principal, right?" I asked. She'd made a friendly dona- tion to the school when we first arrived, so the principal tended to take her calls. "Do you think you could get him to switch one of my classes?"

Olympia looked skeptical. "I've told you before, Kira, physics is going to be very useful to you one day."

Yeah, right.

"It's not that," I said. "I want to switch from

band to art. I hardly think they'll miss my mad triangle skills."

"Art?" Olympia echoed.

"It's for my investigation," I said importantly. Which was true. Getting myself into one of Milo's classes would totally be useful for solving this mystery. It was not just an excuse to spend more time with him—no, sir.

I couldn't do much about the fact that I had no classes with Rowan, since he was a senior like Zach and Tex. But Milo was a junior, like me, and I'd memorized his schedule when I found it conveniently sticking out of his backpack while he paid for the ice cream. Jumping into his fourth period art class seemed like the easiest thing to do. It meant giving up one class with Daniel, but hey, he'd still have me for all the others.

"Hmmm," Olympia said. "All right, I'll call Principal Lovato in the morning and see what I can do."

"Don't change the rest of my schedule," I said. "Just band to art, fourth period. Make sure it's Mrs. Malone's class."

"I hope this isn't another boy thing," Olympia

said, closing her eyes with a sigh.

Well, that was unfair. I'd only had *one* boy thing, and okay, it didn't turn out well, but I thought I deserved a second chance. Besides, if she'd met this boy, she'd understand.

I padded back to the entrance, but as I slid the door aside, Olympia said, "What's happening with that Rowan boy? Did you find out anything about him?"

"I'm working on it," I said. "He's not exactly the most communicative soul."

"Keep trying," she said. "I have a feeling about that one."

"All right," I said, climbing out into the wardrobe. As I clambered out of the basement, I realized there was one more question I should have asked.

Namely: Was this a good feeling or a bad feeling? A *Hey, fellow vampire!* feeling?

Or a *That one might kill us all in our sleep* feeling?

Chapter 11

The next day was Friday, which I love just as much now that I'm a vampire as I did when I was human. I take advantage of the weekends to sleep all day. At least, I do when I'm not in the middle of a murder investigation and, apparently (much to my surprise), dating three boys at once.

It started with Daniel, Friday morning. He was already at his desk when I got to history class, and from the moment I walked in the room I could feel him watching me. I mean, he didn't take his eyes off me as I came down the row to my desk, and I wasn't even wearing anything special—just jeans and a sunny yellow off-the-shoulder shirt and ankle boots. And sunflower earrings. And maybe a couple of tiny yellow butterfly clips in my hair. All right, I might have been feeling a little cheerful when I got dressed. Sure, I had been accused of murder by my family and was wrapped up in a bizarre investigation, but there were such *cute* boys involved. Hey, I try to look on the bright side.

Plus I thought Milo would appreciate the look . . . and judging from the expression on his face, Daniel did, too.

"Morning," I said, sitting down.

"It is now," he said, and then paused, a smile twitching at the corners of his mouth. "I mean— oops. I thought you were going to say 'good morning.'"

"Well, that's what I meant," I said with a smile.

"What are you doing this weekend?" he asked.

Solving a murder, I hope. Maybe breaking into Tex's house. Seducing Rowan and Milo to see if they turn into vampires. And so on.

"Oh, nothin'," I said.

He flipped a pencil between his fingers. "Any chance you'd be interested in dinner tomorrow night?"

I smiled. "I should play hard to get and tell

125

you I have plans, shouldn't I?"

"Too late," he pointed out. "How about I pick you up at nine?"

Ooo, a late dinner—after dark. That was thoughtful . . . or perhaps necessary for him, too.

"Okay, you charmed me into it," I said. I scribbled my address on a scrap of paper and passed it to him. "Should I dress up?"

"Always," he said with his slow smile.

Then Mr. Wright rapped on his desk, and we had to pay attention to history for the rest of the period. So it wasn't until we were walking down the hall to physics that I was able to say, "By the way, I won't be in band today. I'm afraid you'll have to percuss without me."

"What an unfortunate loss," he said. "Why is that?"

"Well, actually I'm switching out of the class," I said, showing him the note I'd picked up from the principal that morning. "I decided I could express myself better with paint than with a pair of cymbals."

Daniel examined the note, looking strangely

126

concerned. "You're leaving the class completely?" he said, like he couldn't believe it.

"I'm sorry," I said. "I've never liked it." This was true. Musical instruments and I were obviously not intended for each other.

"I'll miss you," he said, handing the note back to me.

"Only for fifty minutes," I said. "Then you'll have me back for English."

He nodded, but his smile looked a little forced. "I have bad news, too. I'm afraid I'm going to be busy during lunch today," he said.

"That's okay," I said. "I promised a friend I'd eat with him anyway, so it works out."

Now he looked even *more* disgruntled. Poor Daniel. He acted all mysterious and suave, but maybe he really liked me more than he wanted to let on. After third period, before he went off to do whatever he was "busy" doing during lunch, I tried to make him feel better by touching his arm (well, it sure made *me* feel better) and then leaning up to give him a kiss on the cheek. To my surprise, he caught my wrist as I stepped back.

"Kira," he said in this quiet, intense voice. He pulled me into a doorway, out of the stream of students pouring down the hall. "Be . . ." He paused.

"Be what?" I said.

He laughed ruefully. "I don't know whether to tell you to be good or be careful."

"Daniel, you loon," I said. "I'm just having lunch with a friend. I think we'll all survive."

"I know," he said. "Don't mind me. I just worry sometimes."

"Well, don't worry about me," I said, squeezing his hand. "I can take care of myself." I turned to go, but he caught my hand again and pulled me back. Before I knew what was happening, he put his hands on either side of my face and kissed me.

His lips were soft and cool and serious, like his scent. I barely had time to close my eyes before he broke away and disappeared into the crowd.

I stood there for a moment, feeling strange thrills in my fingertips and toes. *Well, that was sudden.* A real kiss—not the slobbery grope-fest I'd always gotten from Zach. This one was elegant and meaningful, as if the kiss was the main attraction, if that makes sense. With Zach, kissing always seemed like a burdensome truck stop en route to more grabby things. Daniel's kiss was more like my first boyfriend's, although Daniel clearly had a much better idea of what he was doing.

So does that mean we're dating? Doesn't the first kiss usually come after *the first date? Or does sneaking out of school at night after poking around a murder scene somehow count as a date and nobody told me?*

On the other hand, I had dodged a bullet there. If Rowan or Milo had seen him kiss me, it would have been much harder to get close to them. I needed to be careful not to get my guys crossed, at least while they were all still suspects.

Luckily Milo had to eat lunch with the swim team, as he'd informed me yesterday—although he'd made sure to add that if I wanted him to quit the swim team so we could share sandwiches, he'd do it in a heartbeat. I laughed and told him a sacrifice of that magnitude wasn't necessary.

Now the trick was finding Rowan. I had a

hunch he probably ate by himself, and probably not in the cafeteria, although I checked there first, just in case. The usual swirl of noise and mayhem—that many hearts beating so fast in one place is a little much for a vampire to handle. Vivi and I usually ate in the theater, where the drama kids congregate. Vivi is one of the regular stars of the school plays, so she's allowed to bring in whomever she wants, even poor, desperately undramatic me.

So I knew Rowan wouldn't be there, because I'd never seen him there before. Nor was he in the cafeteria or the courtyard (where Milo was sitting at the same table with his swimming friends). I wandered up to the library and peeked into the gym—no luck. Finally, I checked the stairwells. Which turned out to be the right instinct.

Rowan was hunched on the bottom step of the school's back stairwell, the only one that leads down to the basement. I wouldn't have gone all the way down to check, but when I leaned over and peered down the center well, I spotted his backpack leaning against the railing, way at the bottom.

He heard my boots clopping down the stairs toward him and jumped to his feet with a startled expression.

"Sorry, it's just me," I said, holding up my hands. "Kira—remember?"

"Oh," he said, still looking fairly spooked. He sat down again, crumpling his brown bag between his hands.

"I thought I saw you disappear down here," I lied. "Can I join you? What a cool place to get away from everyone." That was a lie, too. The little space at the bottom of the stairwell was dark and pretty dreary. The solid gray door in front of us was labeled BASEMENT. On the plus side (if you're a vampire), absolutely no sun filtered down from the windows on the next level up. The only light was a flickering fluorescent above the basement door, which was sort of unfortunate in terms of me trying to be all cute and attractive. That's a lot harder to do when the light is turning you a washed-out, ghostly mint-green, but I didn't have much choice.

"Yeah, okay," Rowan said, waving his long pale hand at the step beside him.

"How's it going?" I said, sitting down and pulling out my lunch. I peeked sideways at his to see if it was at all suspicious, but it looked like a normal ham sandwich on white bread.

"Fine," he said. It's conversations like these that made me realize why Rowan didn't have girls flocking after him, despite his cool eyes and the tall-brooding-handsome thing.

"Have you ever been in there?" I asked, nodding at the basement door.

He squinted at it for a moment, then rummaged in his bag and pulled out a digital camera. "Yeah," he said, thumbing it on. "I took some shots. Dark and dusty." He scrolled quickly through the images and then handed the camera to me.

The photo on the screen was a close-up of large pipes and the side of a furnace. "Oooh," I said, trying to sound admiring. "How . . . artistic." I hit the arrow to move to the next shot. More pipes. "Can I look at the rest?" Maybe there was a clue in here.

"Sure," he said, taking another bite of his sandwich. As I scrolled through the images, I could tell he was looking surreptitiously at my shoulders. Or possibly my neck. Hmmmm.

Pipes. Pipes. Big pipes. Small pipes. Extremely dusty pipes. A door.

"Are there any other doors to the basement?" I asked.

"Just from the outside," Rowan said. "They always forget to lock it."

Hmmmmm. "Good tip," I said with a smile.

The basement photos ended and I came to one of the horizon at dawn, with the moon still glimmering in the sky. Dark tree branches criss-crossed the sky.

"That's pretty cool," I said.

He nodded. "I don't sleep well. Sometimes I sneak out while my parents are asleep and go for walks really early in the morning."

How early? Midnight early? Vampire early?

I moved to the next photo. The silhouette of the school against the pale orange sky. I hit the arrow key again and gasped.

The image on the screen in front of me . . . was Tex's dead body.

Chapter 12

What does one say to that?

Um, excuse me, why do you have a picture of a corpse on your camera?

But it was even spookier because I could tell from the angle of the shot that the body wasn't surrounded by police tape and curious teenagers.

Rowan had taken this photo earlier that morning . . . *when he was alone with the body.*

A horrified chill crawled across my skin. I was even more scared than I had been when Daniel frightened me at the murder scene. My hands were shaking so badly, I could barely see the image in front of me anymore.

I nearly got up and ran away. Only forcibly reminding myself about my vampire strength made me stay where I was. There wasn't much he could do to me, unless he was hiding a stake in that backpack.

But I also wanted to react like a normal girl; I didn't want to tip him off that I was anything out of the ordinary. Except . . . he wasn't exactly acting like a normal guy. Didn't he think I'd get to this photo eventually? Or was that the idea?

I looked up and met Rowan's eyes. He was watching me. He knew exactly what I'd seen.

He was waiting to see what I did.

"Wow," I said faintly. I decided to opt for a tiny bit of honesty. "I'm a little bit freaked out right now."

"It looks like art, doesn't it?" he said. "The red is so bright against the gray steps, and the composition—you don't even think about what you're seeing at first, because it's such a striking image."

Um, yeah, it's striking . . . it's a DEAD BODY. That was certainly my first thought.

"When did you take this?" I asked. *Was it . . . right after you MUUUUUUURDERED him, perhaps?* I scrolled forward and found two more, similar photos, from closer angles. Then it was back to the basement pipes, and that was all

135

the photos on the camera.

Rowan gave me a sideways look. "I saw it while I was out walking that morning," he said. *It*, I noticed . . . not *him*. "I guess I was the first person to find it. Around five o'clock . . . no one else was up yet. It was really quiet and still and peaceful and then . . . this."

"Didn't you freak out?"

He stared into space for a minute. "Maybe a little."

"What did you do? Are you the one who called the police?" *But not your dad, I guess.* Rowan hadn't told me yet that his dad was a policeman; I only knew that from seeing them together on the morning after the murder.

"No way." Rowan frowned. "I don't trust the cops. Besides, they might have blamed me. Never get them involved if you can help it."

I was processing the Oedipal ramifications of that statement when suddenly he took my free hand and flipped it over in his. His hands were cold but gentle as he traced his fingers over the lines on my palm.

"I don't trust many people," he said.

Seems odd that you'd share your creepy death photos

with a girl you hardly know, then, doesn't it?

He shoved his auburn hair out of his face and looked at me with infinitely sad eyes.

"Such a short life line," he murmured, running his index finger over it again.

I shivered. "No way. I'm going to live forever." *In a manner of speaking.*

"I wonder if Tex felt the same way," Rowan said.

"Maybe everyone does," I said. I decided the direct approach was the way to go with this guy. If he thought we shared a connection . . . "You know," I said, leaning toward him, "I wasn't going to say this to anyone, but it's a relief that someone else is as curious about this murder as I am. I mean, I feel like I'm being morbid if I bring it up with anyone else, but with you, I can be myself. It's like—it's like you understand. You know? I hope that doesn't sound too weird."

"No, no," Rowan said, shaking his head. "I know exactly what you mean. Most people think you're a total psychopath if you say anything about death. But I had a feeling you were different."

"Totally," I said. *Probably helps that I am*

137

dead. Oh, and P.S.: I still think you might be a total psychopath.

"I mean, why should we be afraid to talk about death, right?" Rowan said. "I bet the guy who killed him wishes he could talk about it."

"Um," I said. "Yeah. Totally. I wonder how he feels about it." Meaningful look.

His eyes shifted sideways again. "You want to see something else?"

Um. Do I? "Sure."

He let go of my hand, put away the camera, and rummaged in his bag again. I had no idea what he was about to pull out. A weapon? A vial of Tex's blood? Pictures of his other victims?

Instead he pulled out a cell phone.

Which I guess was a relief.

"Who are you calling?" I asked.

"No, it's not mine," he said, handing it to me. As I took it from him, he said, "It's Tex's."

Oh, fabulous, I thought. *Thank you so much for letting me get my fingerprints all over a dead guy's phone.* "Where did you get it?" I asked, holding it gingerly between my finger and thumb.

"I found it near the body," he said. "It must have fallen out of his pocket when he fell."

Actually, this could be useful evidence. I turned it on and went to the call list.

"I did the same thing," Rowan said, watching me.

So if your number was in here, it's probably gone by now. I checked incoming calls first. There was one at about eight o'clock on the night of the murder—probably just a few hours before his death. The number didn't have a name attached to it.

"That's a pay phone," said Rowan. "Here at the school."

"Pay phones still exist?" I said.

He smiled wryly, which for him was a lot of expression. I was surprised he didn't hurt himself using that many facial muscles. "Well, there's one, at least. Behind the gym."

So someone had called Tex from the school. To arrange a meeting? To lure him to his death? Did that mean the murder was planned? If it wasn't just a random killing, then there must have been a reason the vampire picked Tex.

There weren't many other numbers in the phone; the rest of the incoming calls were from the days before Tex was killed. Photos of cheerleaders or football players were attached to some of them. I glanced at Rowan again. Had he deleted evidence? Was that possible? I'd never tried deleting calls on my cell phone. But Rowan seemed like a tech-savvy kind of guy, at least if you went by the stereotype of computer guys being shy and hanging out in basements. Okay, possibly I was jumping to conclusions just a little.

I was about to open the outgoing calls list when the end-of-lunch bell rang. Rowan snatched the phone out of my hand and stood up.

"Okay, bye," he said, stuffing his things quickly into his backpack.

"Oh, uh . . . thanks for having lunch with me!" I said. "It's great to, you know, finally meet a kindred spirit."

He eyed my cheerful yellow shirt skeptically. "Yeah."

"Hey, what are you doing tonight?" I asked. "I mean, if it's not too last-minute, maybe we could get together and . . . talk some more?"

He shoved his hair out of his eyes and scuffed one boot along the floor. "I'll be at home," he said. "I'm not allowed out on weekends."

"Wow, really?" I said. "That is so sad. Why?" Rowan was already starting to climb the stairs. I scrambled after him, trying to look like I casually hung out with the death-obsessed all the time.

"My dad's a little . . . overprotective," Rowan said.

"Oh, he'll like me," I said. "Parents usually do." Well, they did before the green hair and the multiple piercings; I hadn't met a lot of parents since then. So this would be an interesting experiment. "How about I come over to your place? Is that allowed?"

Rowan paused on the landing and stared at me for a second. "Yeah, okay," he said. "He deserves that."

Whatever that meant.

"Any particular time?" I asked brightly.

"Whatever," he said with a shrug. "6675 Stone Key Circle. Come over whenever."

That was enough invitation for me. I mean that literally. As a vampire, I needed a specific invite like that before I could saunter into his house. And that one was pretty open-ended. Score.

"Bye till later, then," I said, brushing his shoulder with my fingertips as I sailed past him and out into the crowded hallway.

The look in his eyes was sort of haunting—sad and lonely and full of longing for . . . *something*, I wasn't sure what. It stayed with me down the hall, dampening the sunny mood I'd been in when I woke up.

But then I walked through the doors into my new art class and saw Milo—and Milo spotted me.

Is it weird that seeing a guy I'd just met yesterday could make me feel all warm and fizzy inside? Or that his face lit up when he saw me as if he felt the same way? It was like having sunshine poured over my soul, which was exactly what I needed after the dark lunch in the basement with Rowan. I grinned at Milo and wiggled my fingers.

Mrs. Malone didn't bat an eye when I handed her the note. "All right," she said, glancing at it. "Miss November, sit anywhere you like. We're sketching still lifes today. There are blank sketch pads over there."

I grabbed a sketch pad and charcoal pencil. Milo was jerking his head at the stool beside him in a really unsubtle way. I tapped my finger against my lips and pretended to look around at the other tables like I was considering my options. He widened his eyes at me and then pointed his chin at the empty seat again with such vigor that I was afraid he'd break his neck.

"Oh, all right," I said, sitting down next to him with a laugh. "But only because your table has the best still life." The other two guys at the table were already absorbed in their drawings. People all over the room were murmuring to each other as they drew, while Mrs. Malone went around peering at their sketches. She didn't seem to mind if people talked while they worked, which made this the perfect class to have with Milo.

"I know. Have you ever seen a prettier pile of oranges?" Milo said, propping his chin on his hand and gazing at me rapturously. "What are you doing here?"

"I thought I needed some culture," I said with

a mischievous smile. "I figured it would be good for my soul to spend some more time around a really attractive . . . pile of oranges." I should perhaps mention that he looked even cuter than he had yesterday because he was wearing a pair of absolutely adorable glasses. Their thin gold frames brought out the gold flecks in his eyes and made him look all smart and thoughtful and stuff. Yeah, I'll admit it: I'm kind of a sucker for cute boys in glasses.

"If I were a suspicious guy," he said, reaching over to doodle on my sketch pad, "or, you know, a really egocentric one, I might think you were stalking me."

Well . . . yes. "Of course, if you *did* think that highly of yourself, you wouldn't be worth stalking, would you?" I batted my eyelashes at him.

"True," he said. "But if you are stalking me, you know . . . feel free to keep doing that."

"Oh, I don't know," I said. "Stalking would take so much effort. I'd have to figure out where you live—"

"31 Summer Street," he said promptly.

"And which window to stare at—"

"Second floor, the one on the left if you're

144

facing the house," he said. "And it's always open. For you, anyway."

That sounded like an invitation to me! I smiled at him. "Well, maybe if I can fit it in around my other criminal activities."

"How about Sunday?" he said. "I've got some free time to be stalked on Sunday. Or I can ditch my swim meet if you'd rather stalk me on Saturday."

"And deprive the world of shirtless-you time?" I said. "I wouldn't dream of it." *Not to mention I already have a date for Saturday, la la la.* "Sunday would be perfect."

"I like your hair like that," he said, grinning at my butterfly clips.

"I like your glasses," I shot back.

"Oh, yeah?" he said. "I wear contacts on swim days, but these are more comfortable." He wasn't at all self-conscious about them. I liked that even more.

I didn't end up with the world's best sketch of a pile of oranges, but by the end of class, I was more convinced than ever that Milo couldn't be the murderer. He was just too cute. And funny. And dreamy. And adorable. And did I mention funny? I like funny.

Not that I was falling for him or anything. That would be a bad idea. Because if he turned out to be the murderer, then I'd be in love with a murderer, which would suck.

And if he wasn't the murderer, then I'd be in love with a human . . . and that would be even worse.

Chapter 13

One of the things I like about living in Massachusetts is that it starts getting dark pretty early in the fall. I was able to head over to Rowan's at seven o'clock that night, surrounded by shadows.

His house wasn't exactly the Gothic vampire mansion I'd been picturing. I don't know, I guess I'd imagined him living somewhere like Stephen King's house, with gargoyles and a tall spiky fence out front. But instead I found a small, kind of sad-looking ranch house, all on one level with tiny square windows, and a lot of gray concrete visible around the drab beige siding. An unmarked police car sat in the driveway.

It occurred to me for the first time that if Rowan was a vampire, then surely the rest of his family was, too. It would be tough for parents not to notice that their kid suddenly had developed fangs and a really serious blood fixation. Rowan's dad certainly knew *something* was wrong with his son, if his behavior at the crime scene had been any indication.

I had debated changing my outfit, but I didn't want to look like I was trying too hard. Besides, I hoped that cheerful sunflower earrings would send a "nonthreatening!" message to Rowan's parents. Or his vampire family, or whomever I was about to meet in there. As I pulled open the screen door and rang the bell, I wondered if this was a bad idea. If they were vampires, and they thought I was onto Rowan, what might they do to me?

Too late. The front door swung open. Rowan's dad was standing there, still in his police uniform.

He stared at me with the same spooky expression Rowan had, like I was wearing a garland of skulls around my neck or something.

Evidently brilliant conversational skills, such as the ability to say *hello*, ran in the family.

"Hi, there," I said with a wide smile. *Look*

how harmless I am! "Are you Rowan's dad? I'm Kira. He said I could stop by—I hope I'm not interrupting dinner or anything." I peered at his face, but there weren't any telltale bloodstains around his mouth.

"No, we—no—who did you say you were?"

"Kira. Kira November." I stuck out my hand but he didn't move. "Rowan and I go to school together and I'm new and he's been so nice and I hardly know anyone so it's great to have a friend—" I figured if I babbled, that would help fill up all the awkward silence.

"Rowan has a friend?" This came from a new voice, as a pallid, wispy middle-aged woman appeared behind the policeman. "Oh, hello, dear," she said over her husband's elbow. "Albert, don't be rude. Come on in, sweetheart."

Hmm. Someone hasn't been trained in anti-vampire protocol. "Thanks, ma'am," I said as she tugged her husband aside so I could edge into the hall-way. Rowan's dad was frowning at me in a way I don't like to be frowned at, especially by police officers.

"Rowan!" his mom called. "Your friend is here!" She patted my hand. "Rowan never gets any visitors. He's always been a quiet boy, but ever since we moved, it seems like he's always locked up in that room of his."

"Donna," said Rowan's dad in a low, warning kind of voice.

Rowan appeared from a room at the end of the hall, like a spectral wraith rising from the mist. He'd taken off his hoodie, and his pale, skinny arms stuck out of his T-shirt. His hair was mussed and he looked sleepy, as if he'd just woken up.

"Do you know this girl?" Rowan's dad asked sternly.

"Albert!" said Rowan's mom.

"Yeah," Rowan said, combing his hair with his fingers. "We've been hanging out. So? Isn't that what you want for me? A normal life?"

Albert's smile was strained. "Perhaps now isn't a good time," he said to me.

"It's a fine time," Rowan said. "Kira, come see my room."

I sidled nervously toward him. "Er . . . nice to meet you," I said to Rowan's parents.

"You too, dear," said Donna.

"Keep the door open!" Albert barked as

Rowan led me into his room. Okay, *that* wasn't sinister at all.

In response, Rowan slammed the door behind us. "I hate him," he said. He leaned on the door like he was listening to see if his dad would keep fighting. But there was no further sound from the other side.

I was sort of hoping for a nice, obvious coffin in the middle of the room, but there was nothing like that. There wasn't a real bed, either; instead a twin mattress lay in the middle of the floor, covered in tangled black sheets with a threadbare, blue plaid blanket crumpled on top and one flat pillow at the end. Rowan stepped around me and shoved the mattress over to the wall, shaking out the blanket and covering the sheets with it.

There were more windows than I'd expect in a vampire's room—three of them—but I remembered that tall, thick hedges grew at this end of the house, probably blocking all the light even if Rowan hadn't kept his shades drawn. I also noticed that two of the shades were taped to the window frame with thick black duct tape. Keeping out the tiny slivers of daylight?

A chest of drawers stood on the same wall as the closet door, which was ajar, but it didn't look like Rowan used either one very much, as clothes were strewn across the plain beige carpet and piled high on the wooden chair next to the desk. I was actually surprised to see so many clothes; from what I'd seen of Rowan so far, I thought perhaps he owned only one pair of black jeans, one black hooded sweatshirt, and an assortment of dark T-shirts. But from here I could see at least three pairs of black jeans, so I suppose that was reassuring.

The walls were covered in photographs, all of them stuck up with jagged scraps of more black duct tape. I looked at them while Rowan tossed his clothes into the closet.

Lots of pictures of the moon; thankfully, no human corpses, although there were a few close-ups of roadkill that I could really have lived forever without seeing, thanks very much. Several shots were of blurry backgrounds through windows and rain, so all you could see were the drops of rain on the glass with fuzzy shapes behind them. There were no photographs of Rowan or his family—or any people, in fact.

"Where are all the sunny shots of the Golden Gate Bridge?" I asked with a smile.

He squinted at me. "What?"

"None of these look like San Francisco," I said, pointing to the photographs. "Didn't you take any pictures while you were living there?"

He ran his fingers through his hair again. "Uh, no. I didn't feel like it." He sat down at his desk and moved his mouse to wake up the screensaver. I noticed that he had a solitaire game up on his computer, which seemed a little lame.

I turned around and saw that he had a black sheet pinned over something on the back of the door. "What's under here?" I asked, going to lift it up.

"Don't!" he snapped. I froze, and he took a deep breath. "Don't do that."

"Okay." I took a step back. "Why?"

"It's a mirror," he said. "I just don't like mirrors."

Oh, RRRREALLY?

Part of me wanted to whip off the sheet and see if I could see him in the mirror. That would answer the whole vampire question pretty definitively. On the other hand, if he *was* human, and he realized that he couldn't see *me* . . . that would take some explaining.

"What's wrong with mirrors?" I asked, sitting down on the mattress, since there wasn't anywhere else to sit. I leaned my back against the wall and rested my elbows on my knees.

"I don't like looking at myself," he said, clicking on the solitaire game.

"You should," I said. "You're totally cute."

He tilted his head slowly at me. "No one's ever said that to me before."

Yeah, most likely because you're also weird as all get out. "Well, I'm very observant," I said, crossing my ankles and leaning back on my hands. "I also observed that your dad is kind of scary. Did you know that?"

Rowan made a little growling noise in his throat. "He's a jerk. He doesn't trust me. He says he does, but he treats me like a dangerous animal."

"That sucks," I said, studying his profile as

he stared at the computer screen. "Why is he like that?"

"He's a cop, I guess." Rowan shrugged. "He has a pretty strict idea of right and wrong, but I think it's kind of messed up. I can't do anything without getting this *look* from him, like he has no idea who I am. Whatever."

"Does he know anything about Tex's murder?" I asked. "I mean, since he's a cop."

Rowan snorted. "He won't talk about it. Thinks it's bad for my head. He's one of those people who doesn't understand." He gave me that sad look again. "Not like you."

"I only talked to Tex once," I said. "My brother Zach and I were at my locker, having a fight—that happens a lot. And Tex came up to us and poked Zach's shoulder and said, 'Is this punk bothering you, little lady?' and Zach was like, 'Don't even bother, Tex, she's a frigid—' and then I kicked him in the shins and he fell over and Tex was like, 'Dude, your sister is hot but scary,' and Zach was like, 'Tell me about it,' and I was like, 'You two should just date each other; you'd be a cute couple,' and Tex was like, 'Aw, but the ladies would be so disappointed.'

And that was it. I don't know, he seemed doofy, but not as obnoxious as some of those guys."

"They're all the same," Rowan said. "Meat-heads. You only need to get shoved into a locker by one of them to know what they're all like."

"Did Tex do that to you?" I asked. "Shove you into a locker?" *Was that your motive . . . for MURRRRRDER?*

"Nah," Rowan said. "He hit me with a vol-leyball a few times in gym, that's all. But only 'cause I was there and it was easy. I don't think he knew I was alive. If you asked him who I was, he wouldn't have a clue." I listened for undercurrents of bitterness in his voice, but I didn't hear any. Either they weren't there, or he was a good actor.

He swiveled around to look at me. "I don't mind, if that's what you're thinking. I like being invisible."

"I guess it's useful for a photographer," I said, waving at the wall. *And also for a vampire.*

"Want to see my poem?" he asked. Without waiting for an answer, he opened a drawer in his desk and pulled out a locked metal box. He turned it away from me so I couldn't see the combination as he opened it. I spotted several papers inside, but he quickly pulled out the top sheet and closed the box with a snap. He spun the lock and hid the box inside his desk again.

"Here," he said, coming over to the mattress. He sat down beside me and handed me the poem. His sleeve brushed my bare arm, and our knees were practically touching.

The poem covered both sides of the page. As one might expect from an epic titled "Blood," it was written in red ink with splotches everywhere, and it was mostly long, scribbled lines about how red and warm and sticky and hot blood is. *Um, gross.* Nothing about how blood tasted, though, I noticed. But it did feel like it had been written by someone who'd been close to a lot of blood. There was a line that went "blood, blood fiery against my fingertips." Boy, his dad would not be pleased if he found out Rowan had literally gotten Tex's blood on his hands.

"This is really—" I started to say, but suddenly Rowan leaned over and kissed me.

I guess I should have expected that. This is what happens when you flirt with boys, especially unstable boys. And I *was* interested to see if his fangs came out while he was kissing me.

But on the other hand, it was really awkward. He kind of missed my mouth at first, and then he tried to pull me around to face him, and then he was leaning into me too much and I didn't have anywhere to put my arms to support myself. It was wicked uncomfortable. Plus he almost immediately tried to stick his tongue between my teeth, which is a kissing technique I've never fully understood, frankly.

And I couldn't help thinking about Milo and Daniel, and how I'd much rather be kissing one of them. It was bad enough to be flirting with two guys I really did like; adding in Rowan suddenly felt like cheating. This murder investigation stuff was *complicated*.

"Hey, wait," I said, putting my hands on his chest and pushing him away. "This is a little fast for me."

"But I thought you liked me," Rowan said. He put his hand on my knee and leaned in again.

"Yeah, well," I said, dodging, "but we just met, and—"

His hand gripped my knee surprisingly tightly. "Oh, God," he said. He let go of me all at once and buried his head in his hands. "I'm an idiot. I ruin everything."

"No, don't say that," I said, feeling a twinge of guilt.

Suddenly the door flew open and I nearly jumped out of my skin. Rowan's dad glowered down at us. All I could think was *Thank God he didn't walk in one minute earlier.* Although I imagine we still looked pretty suspicious, side by side on the mattress like that.

"I think you'd better go," he said to me.

"DAD," Rowan said angrily.

"It's okay. I've got stuff to do," I said, scrambling to my feet. "See you Monday, Rowan?"

He scowled at his bare feet and didn't answer.

Albert followed me down the hall to the front door. As I reached for the handle, he stopped me with one hand on my elbow. It was a gentle grip, firm but not scary. I looked at him in surprise.

"I'm sorry," he said. "About Rowan, I mean. I hope you won't think—I hope you'll be kind to him. He's having a rough time right now, and he sometimes says things he shouldn't."

"It's okay," I said awkwardly.

"Just don't believe everything he says," Rowan's dad went on. "If he sounds like he's talking crazy or anything—I mean, you let me know, all right? If he says anything that sounds weird, or if he talks like he did anything crazy, or anything like that. Don't take him seriously."

I didn't know who was more spooked, me or poor old Albert. I glanced over his shoulder and saw another mirror in the living room, over the fireplace, also covered in a black sheet like a shroud.

"I'll let you know," I said. "He seems all right to me." Well, apart from the corpse pictures and the overall moodiness and the potentially being a vampire, anyway. "Maybe a little sad."

Albert's eyes were sad, too. "Have a good night," he said, opening the door for me.

I hurried down the driveway to the sidewalk, feeling a shiver run along my spine. When I glanced back, I saw movement in three different windows—three faces peering at me through the blinds, each from a different room. Donna and Albert dropped the blinds when I saw them, but Rowan stayed put, staring at me with those deep, dark blue eyes as I walked away down the street.

Chapter 14

𝓘 needed a strong dose of normalcy when I got home, so I kidnapped the portable phone to call Vivi. She's the one real friend I've made since moving to Massachusetts, mainly because she's kind of a space cadet and would never notice anything weird about me. I think even if my fangs popped out in front of her, she'd be like, "Dude, something's wrong with your makeup—oh, and by the way, did you hear who's going to be on *Dancing with the Stars* this year?"

This is one of the many things I like about her.

Crystal was watching TV by herself when I went into the den to snag the phone. "Where's Bert?" I asked.

"I don't know," she said. "I thought he went

upstairs with Zach a while ago, but I also heard someone go out the back door, so maybe that was him."

"Is everything okay?" I asked.

"Oh, yeah," she said. "He's just been acting kinda weird lately. Kinda distant, you know? It's probably just money stuff, though—he gets all wrapped up in that kind of thing."

Bert always seemed a little weird and distant to me, but I didn't point this out to her. He's still a really nice guy, even when he's odd.

I didn't run into either of my vampire parents as I headed for my room; possibly they were still asleep, since it was only early evening. I didn't want to see them anyway. They'd ask if I'd found the murderous vampire yet, and I wasn't sure that my creepy feelings plus Rowan's corpse photo would add up to enough evidence for them. But I also wasn't sure I wanted to keep investigating him, either. Not if there would be any more tongue-kissing involved.

Vivi picked up her phone at once. "Kira!" she squealed. She didn't exactly sound "shattered" or "overcome."

"Hey, lady," I said, lying down on my bed.

"I miss you. School is wicked boring without you."

"You big liar," she said. "I hear you've been having *way* too much fun in my absence."

"Me?" I said innocently. "What are you talking about?"

"I'm talking about *two* cute boys!" she cried. "First of all, who's the new mystery guy? Ruby says he looks just like Will Smith."

I smiled. "I'm not telling you anything. You deserve to suffer for abandoning me all week."

"*Hello*, I was *recovering*," Vivi said. "Don't torture me, Kira! Tell me about him! Is he as hot as everyone says?"

"Who's everyone?" I asked. "Why are you talking to all these other people instead of to me?"

"I've called you like fifty times!" Vivi cried, outraged. "Didn't Zach tell you?"

"Of course not," I said. "Big lummox." On the other hand, I didn't give him a lot of opportunity to pass along messages, considering that I practically jumped out the window whenever I heard him coming.

"He's probably all broken up about Tex, too,"

Vivi said melodramatically. I've mentioned that she's an aspiring actress, right? "I bet the heart-ache distracted him."

"Oh, yeah, that's Zach," I said. "He's just so sensitive."

She missed my sarcasm entirely. "You are dodging the question, missy," she said. "*Tell me* about the hot mystery boy!"

"All right," I said, laughing. "But there's not much to tell. His name is Daniel. I met him the day before he started at Luna, so I've been showing him around—that's all."

"Yeah, sure," she said. "And what about Milo Sparks?"

"Sheesh, you do know everything, don't you?" I said. "For someone who's been lying in bed all week, you're remarkably well informed." I was glad she didn't seem to know about Rowan, though. I unzipped my book bag and pulled out my sketch pad. Just thinking about Milo and Daniel made me smile.

"What did you *do* to him?" Vivi demanded. "He's famously unapproachable! No one's ever been able to date him! And now I hear that he's completely smitten with my best friend and she hasn't even told me about it!"

"I don't know about smitten," I said, blushing. "And I'm sure he's had a girlfriend before."

"Not in this town, he hasn't," she said. "Ruby's been trying to get his attention for two years with no luck."

Bet she never tried falling in a pool, I thought. "I'm just lucky, I guess."

"Lucky and hot," Vivi said. "At this rate, you're going to have all the girls in school dyeing their hair green. Whatever it takes to get your luck with boys."

I found the page Milo had been doodling on. He'd written *Kira loves Milo* and *Mrs. Kira Sparks* and his phone number with a heart around it, as if I were a sixth-grader with a crush and had written all that myself. I laughed.

"So which one do you like better?" Vivi demanded.

"Well, Daniel is smoldering-sexy-hot," I said. "He has that whole 'man of mystery' thing happening. But Milo is cute, *and* he's really funny."

"Can I have whichever one you don't want?" she asked wistfully.

"Aw, what about Alejandro?" Her boyfriend

wasn't exactly terrible-looking himself.

"Oh, he's in a mood because he doesn't understand why I needed to take three days off to mourn Tex. It's like he has no idea how sensitive and delicate I am. Hey, are you going to the memorial service tomorrow?"

"Memorial service?" I echoed. "Didn't they do that at school?"

"Well, this is the real one," she said. "It's tomorrow night at seven, at the football field. I think practically the whole town is going to be there. I heard his mom and dad are going to dedicate something to him, like a tree or a trophy case or something. And then the whole town is invited back to their house for a wake on Sunday."

I perked up. "The whole town?" *That would seem to encompass any vampires in town, wouldn't it?*

"Yeah, it's in the paper," she said. "Open invitation. So you want to go?"

"Oh," I said. "No, I think I probably won't—I mean, I didn't really know him, and it's kind of weird, you know?" *Plus if everyone will be at the football field . . . and I suddenly have an open invitation to their house . . . then that would be the perfect time to sneak into Tex's room and search for clues.*

"Oh, man," Vivi said. "Are you sure? We could go out for milkshakes afterward or something. I mean, like, sad, appropriately somber milkshakes. Oooh, maybe you could bring Zach."

I made a face. "I'm sorry. I can't," I said. "I kind of . . . have a date."

"I knew it!" she shrieked. "I leave you alone for two days and suddenly you have this crazy love life! It's not fair! Okay, who's it with? Where are you going? And most important, what are you going to wear?"

See, that's why I like Vivi. She can take a date with a possible bloodthirsty vampire and focus on what's really important. We spent the next two hours talking about outfits and boys, and by the time I hung up, all the spooky emotional cobwebs left over from my encounter with Rowan's family had been swept away.

Not only that, but now I had a plan. While the town was busy at Tex's memorial service, I'd be climbing into his bedroom window and snooping around for clues. I figured two hours before my date with Daniel was plenty of time.

Just to be safe, though, I dressed for the date ahead of time. Which is how I found myself standing in Tex's backyard at seven thirty on Saturday night, trying to figure out how to get through a prickly hedge thicket without ripping my tights. Enormous hemlocks blocked the windows all the way around the house, which if you asked me was downright unfriendly. Although perhaps I should have known that breaking into a house in a dark green crushed velvet minidress wasn't exactly the best idea.

I put my hands on my hips and glared at the windows. There must be another way in. I'd checked the garage door, but it had a number touch pad to open it, so that didn't help me.

I lifted the mat under the back door. Nothing. I jumped up and ran my hand along the top of the door frame, which was both fruitless and dirty. Wiping off the dirt, I checked any might-be-fake-looking rocks around the door, but none of them had keys hidden inside. Of course, I could pull the door open with my vampire strength, but I didn't want to be all obvious about it. Wilhelm would definitely not be pleased about any more suspiciously vampire-like criminal scenes.

I studied the door again and finally spotted the cat flap.

Oh, universe. Why do you make me do these things?

Yes, I actually am that small, luckily—although for the sake of my dress and tights, it would have been nice to be a few inches smaller in every direction. I wriggled and shoved and squeezed and held my breath, and finally I popped out the other side and sprawled onto the Harrisons' cold kitchen floor.

The house was really still. I could hear a grandfather clock *tick-tocking* in the hall. Dishes were sitting in the sink like nobody had the energy to even stack them in the dishwasher. I crawled to my feet and headed for the stairs, peeking into each room as I went by. A spacious white living room, tasteful and austere in comparison to ours. An elegant dining room that looked like it was rarely used. A small room with brown leather couches arranged around a TV—no doubt this was where Tex and his dad were exiled to watch football, while his mom and older sister genteelly ruled over the clean living room. I'd read about his sister, Caprice, in the paper; she'd come home from college for the funeral.

I padded up the stairs and opened doors until I found the bedroom that was unmistakably Tex's. Everything screamed sports: cheerleader calendars, Patriots bedsheets, Red Sox banners and lampshades and rug. I stepped in and closed the door behind me with a quiet *snick*.

It was obvious that his parents hadn't touched anything in here since the day he died. His bed-sheets were thrown back like he'd just gotten up; a basketball lay discarded on the floor next to a pair of sneakers. A screensaver of Angelina Jolie pictures kept shifting across his desktop computer monitor. Classy.

A thought struck me: Why hadn't the police been here yet? Or if they had, they'd been very careful not to move anything. Maybe they were waiting until after the funeral to disturb the family. *I* don't know; I'm not the police. I was just doing their job for them.

In case you're wondering, by the way, I wasn't being a total idiot. I had on elbow-length black gloves and my hair was clipped back, so I was at least making some effort not to leave any stray

DNA lying around. Although if they did find anything to put in their system, the result would come back as a dead girl named Phoebe Tanaka, so my guess is they'd figure there was a glitch in their technology and throw it out anyway.

I sat down at Tex's desk and moved the mouse on the Red Sox mouse pad. His email inbox popped onto the screen. It was creepy to see a couple of new messages at the top, clearly from people who hadn't heard the news yet. There was also one from Ruby, Vivi's friend. I didn't open it, but I could see the message in the preview box: *I miss you, Tex.* I didn't open any of the new emails; I figured that would be pretty suspicious, too.

At the bottom of the screen I saw a couple of other tabs: an English essay and the beginning of a blog entry. Curious, I clicked on the blog.

It was dated the evening of the murder, around seven thirty, but had not yet been posted. I guess he'd started it, and then the call from whoever was at the school had interrupted him. Although I could also see from his email that he'd last checked his messages at around eleven o'clock, so he hadn't left for the school until late at night, which fit with the official report in the paper that he'd died around midnight.

I scanned the unposted blog, and my blood ran cold.

He knew. Tex knew.

The blog entry said:

Guys, you're never going to believe what I saw today! Prepare for your minds to be blown. THERE IS A VAMPIRE IN OUR TOWN! Seriously! I caught him today. I know! Yeah, me! I saw a vampire! I know you're like, Whoa, what? Tex is crazy! but it's true. I saw him in the mirror—actually, I didn't see him in the mirror. He was standing right in front of it BUT THERE WAS NOTHING THERE! Total vampire, dudes! I bet if I wanted to, I could get him to make me a vampire, too, but then Notre Dame might take back that football scholarship, am I right? Ha ha! So what do I do? Do you all want to know who it is? Should I reveal his identity? Post a comment and tell me what you think!

I was glad I was sitting down. Now *here* was a motive for murder. Forget getting shoved into a locker; if a vampire thought Tex was about to expose him, it wasn't entirely surprising he'd throw the guy out a window. Not that that made it okay, of course.

So who was it? It must have been someone Tex saw on Tuesday. Did that mean I could cross Daniel off the suspect list? But it was possible they'd met somehow. . . . I couldn't exactly take Daniel's word on the matter. On the other hand, Rowan had mentioned that he had gym class with Tex; maybe Tex had noticed his lack of a reflection in the locker room.

Far be it from me to tamper with a police investigation under normal circumstances, but in this case, tampering was a case of life or death (at least, I was pretty sure Wilhelm would think so). I deleted the blog entry, and then I went into the computer's history and deleted any traces of it I could find. Probably not the most foolproof method, but hopefully if it wasn't sitting there staring the police in the face when they checked the computer, then they wouldn't pay much attention to it if they ever did find it.

I was about to go back through Tex's emails again when suddenly I heard a noise.

It wasn't a loud noise—human hearing wouldn't have picked it up at all. But to my vampire ears, it was crystal clear.

Footsteps were coming up the stairs.

Someone else was in the house.

Chapter 15

𝓘 dove into the closet, which I realized right away was a mistake because (a) what a totally obvious place to hide, and (b) boys' clothes smell something *awful*. I guessed I was knee-deep in dirty laundry, but I didn't have time to find a better spot. I could hear the footsteps coming down the hall, straight toward Tex's room.

I crouched down and pulled the closet door almost all the way shut, leaving myself only a tiny crack to peer out of.

The bedroom door opened. A figure stood silhouetted in the light from the hall for a brief moment. Then whoever it was stepped into the room and shut the door. Like me, he or she didn't turn on the light. Like me, the newcomer stood there for a long moment, staring around the room. I could see only a faint outline of the person's shape in the glow from the computer monitor.

The computer! I'd forgotten to turn the screensaver back on! That would have taken too long anyway. Did this person know that there should be sexy Angelina Jolie pictures spinning across the screen right now?

There was an excruciatingly long pause. I was very glad I didn't have a heartbeat, because I was sure it would be hammering fit to wake the dead. As it was, I had to clutch my hands together to keep from shaking.

Was it someone who lived here? His mom or dad? How would I ever explain what I was doing in their son's bedroom? I wondered what happened to vampires in prison. Was there an underground blood network to keep me alive?

Or was it Tex's killer, come to erase evidence like I had just done? What would he do if he found me in here . . . and knew that I'd seen him?

The figure took a step forward. The pale blue light from the computer illuminated his face.

I couldn't help it. I gasped.

He whipped around with a startled expression

as I threw open the closet door.

"What are you doing here?" I demanded.

"*Me?*" Daniel said indignantly. "What are *you* doing here?"

"*I* am solving a murder," I said. "*You* are obviously up to no good."

"No, *I'm* solving a murder," he said. "And this is looking very fishy for you, young lady."

"Nuh-uh!" I cried. "You're the fishy one! Skulking about, giving people heart attacks!"

"Well, if you weren't *lurking* in the dark where you're not supposed to be, then you wouldn't be so easily frightened, would you?" he said. "And I wasn't *skulking*."

"Yeah, well, I wasn't *lurking*."

We glared at each other for a moment, nose to nose . . . well, technically, nose to really nice pecs, since he was substantially taller than me. I was pleased to see he was wearing another button-down shirt with most of the buttons undone. I don't know a lot of guys who wander around dressed like that, but on Daniel it was a look I didn't mind. At all.

Distracted? Who, me?

I stared up into his perfect, dark brown eyes,

which were flashing with anger. His breathing was quick and shallow, and his hands were trembling a little bit. What was he thinking? Did he suspect I was the murderer? Or was *he* really the murderer, and he'd realized he was busted? Was he about to pop out a pair of fangs and try to bite me?

I decided the best way to distract him was to kiss him. Or maybe I just really wanted to.

Perhaps he had the same idea at the same time, because it seemed like he grabbed my arms and pulled me to him just as I was leaning up toward his lips.

This wasn't the sweet, elegant kiss he'd given me in the school hallway. This was passion and fire. I ran my hands up his back under his shirt, and he made a tiny sound deep in his throat.

For a moment I thought about throwing him down on the bed and having my way with him right there, but then I was like, *Wow, that would be inappropriate.* Plus who knows when was the last time Tex changed the sheets, and just imagine his parents walking in on *that*, and surely there's somewhere more romantic we could—

Daniel pushed me away from him. "This is a dangerous game," he said, pointing at me. No fangs had magically appeared, I was disappointed to note. Of course, I was much better at controlling mine by this point, so my face also gave nothing away. If he was a vampire, that just meant he'd had experience with this—but I didn't like that thought either.

"What game?" I said, adjusting my dress. That motion seemed to get his attention in a different way. He blinked at my tall boots like he was trying hard not to look at my cleavage. "I'm not playing any games," I continued. "All I see here is you messing up my murder investigation."

"What?" he exploded. "You're the one who's messing up *my*—" He stopped and pressed his fingers to his forehead. "Why are you trying to solve this?" he asked slowly.

Yeah, right. You can tell me the truth first, mister. "Because I'm plucky?" I tried with a winning smile. "I'm just a crime-fighting kind of gal?"

He glared at me.

"Okay, I'll be honest," I said. "It's because I've watched every episode of *Veronica Mars*, like, three hundred times, and I totally want to be her."

He looked at his watch. "We don't have time for this. We have to get out of here soon."

"How did you get in?" I asked curiously.

"The back door was unlocked," he said. He tilted his head at me. "Isn't that how you got in?"

This conversation sounded familiar. Only this time I felt a lot more silly. I hadn't even tried the doorknob. I was an absolute moron.

"Er . . . no," I admitted. "I went through the cat flap."

Daniel hid a smile.

"Don't you dare say, 'That explains the hair,'" I said fiercely.

"Wouldn't dream of it," he said, and glanced around. "Well, did you find anything?"

"No," I lied. "I'd only been here a couple minutes when I heard you." I nodded at the computer screen. Daniel sat down in the chair and studied Tex's inbox. I watched over his shoulder as he tapped a couple of keys.

A box popped up with Tex's last IM conversation in it.

"Hmmm," Daniel said. "Do you know who

Pire-O-Maniac66 is?"

"No," I said, leaning in to read the chat. It seemed pretty innocuous.

Tex had written: *Hey, man. I'm bored. You?*

Pire-O-Maniac66: *Same.*

Tex: *Want to play basketball?*

Pire-O-Maniac66: *Yeah, sure.*

Tex: *Awesome. Meet me at the school in thirty.*

"Riveting," I said. "The life of Tex Harrison was full of novelty and excitement."

"But that was the afternoon before the murder," Daniel pointed out. "Maybe he had a fight with the guy while they were playing basketball."

Or maybe they were both standing in front of a mirror afterward . . . in the guys' locker room?

"Yeah, maybe," I said. "Although you'd have to be pretty psycho to kill a guy for scoring more goals than you."

Daniel just looked at me.

"What?" I said. "Is that not the phrase? Scoring more hoops?"

Daniel shook his head and closed the chat window. "I don't see anything else," he said. "We'd better go."

I wondered if he planned to sneak back again

sometime without me, but I didn't care. I'd already found a *way* better clue than he would. *Take that, Mr. Amateur Detective.*

We hurried down the stairs and slipped out the back door, checking that the coast was clear before we darted around to the sidewalk in front of the house.

As we walked away down the street, I saw a car drive past with three people in it—people I recognized from the photos in Tex's house.

"Whew," Daniel said as he spotted them, too. He pulled out a handkerchief—a real handkerchief!—and dabbed at his forehead, just like a guy in a Jane Austen movie. "That was close."

"So," I said, patting my hair into place and smiling up at him, "does this date still include dinner?"

Chapter 16

Believe it or not, Daniel and I managed to have a very civilized date after that. You might think it'd be a little awkward, each of us being so very suspicious and all, but we just avoided the topics of murder and amateur sleuthing, and everything went surprisingly well. I think the slinky minidress helped cheer him up. Plus he took me to a steakhouse, which is a pretty direct route to my heart now that I'm a hard-core carnivore.

Of course I spent the whole time wondering why Daniel was investigating the murder. But I knew bringing it up would make Daniel ask me questions, too . . . the kind I wasn't about to answer.

I stayed up the rest of the night organizing and reorganizing my clue sheets, in the hope that staring at them in different ways would give me the answer I was looking for. I fell asleep shortly before dawn.

Which is why I was not entirely thrilled when Zach banged on my bedroom door six hours later, at eleven in the morning.

"GO AWAY!" I yelled from under the covers.

"What's that?" he called through the door.

"Leave me alone, Zach!"

"All right," he said with a note of glee in his voice. "I'll just tell him you don't want to see him."

"Yeah," I mumbled into my pillow. A moment later, I sat bolt upright in bed. "Wait, *who*?" I bellowed. "Him WHO?"

I knew he could hear me, because I could still hear him, humming smugly as he trotted off down the stairs. But he didn't respond.

Dadblasted . . .

I jumped out of bed and ran to my dresser. I sleep in a tank top and boxer shorts, and there's no "him" I could think of that I'd want to see me like that. But I had to get downstairs quickly, so I had a critical choice to make: (a) find a sweatshirt, (b) brush my hair, or (c) put on pants. If you'd ever seen me first thing in the morning, you'd understand why I picked (b). I ran a brush quickly through my hair, flung open the door, and raced downstairs after Zach.

"Sorry," Zach was saying as he swung the front door shut. I seized the handle and yanked it out of his grasp.

Milo was standing on the front step, looking disgustingly perky and rugged and gorgeous and awake for that hour of the morning.

"Uh-oh," he said when he saw me.

"You better believe 'uh-oh'!" I cried. "Do you know what time it is?"

"Almost noon?" he said with an apologetic smile.

"*Not even* noon!" I said. "I'm afraid this relationship is doomed."

"Would it help if I said you look really cute in your pajamas?" Milo said. I glanced down at the penguins snoozing in sunglasses on my boxer shorts. My black tank top said *Wake me when there's pancakes* in white letters across the chest.

"No, because I'm pretty sure you'd be lying," I said.

"I'm not!" Milo protested. "I think they're adorable."

"AHEM." Behind me, Zach cleared his throat pointedly. "If you guys are done making everybody sick, could we close the door, please? Milo, dude, either come in or go away."

I glared at Zach. Talk about not knowing your antivampire protocol! My *one* chance to find out if Milo needed an invitation into the house, and Zach blew it.

Milo gave me puppy-dog eyes. "Is it okay? Can I come in?" he asked. He held up a paper bag. "Would muffins help?"

"Hmm," I said. "Depends. What kind?"

"Banana chocolate chip."

"Ooooh, in *that* case," I said, holding the door open. As Milo came in, I glanced past him and saw his car in the driveway. Why was he awake in the middle of the day? Did that mean he definitely wasn't a vampire—or was he just trying to act like a regular human for my benefit?

Zach followed us into the kitchen with a

sullen look on his face. "So why are you here?" he growled at Milo.

"Zach, don't you have a calculus test to finish?" I said pointedly.

"I'm done with it," he said, hopping onto one of the kitchen stools with a definite *I'm not going anywhere* attitude.

"Sorry about my *brother*," I said to Milo. Zach scowled even more at the b-word.

"No worries, Zach is cool," Milo said, giving Zach a smile that was not returned. See, if there was any question that something was wrong with Zach, this had just answered it. It's simply unnatural to resist a smile like Milo's.

Crystal poked her blond head around the door. "Did I hear someone say muffins?" she asked. I knew she must have been asleep when he said it, but Crystal is like me—she can sense food from a mile away, and will even get up in the middle of the day for it.

"Milo, this is my sister, Crystal," I said. "I should warn you this is a house full of ravening wolves, so I hope you brought enough muffins to save yourself."

"Let's find out," he said, opening the bag. I handed him a plate and he shook about a dozen muffins onto it. My mouth dropped open.

"Did you *make* those?"

"Um . . . yeah," he said. "Is that weird? Do you think I'm less manly now?"

"Yes," growled Zach.

"Mmmblvvttwsmph," Crystal said around a mouthful of muffin. She'd practically used vampire super-speed to dive on them.

"I think you're the manliest, most attractive muffin-maker I've ever met," I said, slipping my arms around Milo's waist and giving him a hug. Zach looked like he was about to throw up.

"I can never find muffins that are both banana and chocolate chip," Milo explained, putting his arm around my shoulders, "so I figure I have to make them myself."

"Okay, all is forgiven," I said. "I can learn to love a muffin man, even if he does keep crazy hours."

Milo and Crystal laughed. Zach, not so much.

"Have you guys seen Bert?" Crystal asked,

nibbling the edges of her muffin. "I woke up and he was gone."

"Nope, sorry," I said. Zach shook his head.

"So weird," she said. "I checked all the rooms. He must be out somewhere."

"That's Crystal's husband," I explained to Milo as she wandered out of the kitchen.

"Where are your parents?" Milo asked.

"Slee—" Zach started.

"Out," I said, kicking him hard under the table. What kind of normal grown-ups would be asleep at nearly noon on a Sunday? "So what are we doing today, now that someone has so rudely awakened me and everything?"

"Well," Milo said, "how do you feel about the beach?"

My face must have revealed my true feelings before I could speak, because immediately he went, "Because I think it's terrible. Blech, who likes the beach, am I right? I hate the beach. Totally hate it. Yuck."

I laughed. "Besides, a beach in Massachusetts in early October?"

"Yeah, okay, worst idea ever," Milo said agreeably. "You know what is good, though,

190

is . . . going to the mall?" My nose had barely wrinkled before he said, "Just kidding! I hate the mall, too. Worst place ever."

I used to like the mall, but you have no idea how many mirrors there are in your average mall until suddenly your life depends upon avoiding them. This is the one thing Vivi and I argue about, because she thinks it's fundamentally un-American to hate malls. She keeps saying to me, "But you dress so well! You *must* love shopping! I don't understand!"

Sadly, nowadays I do all my clothes shopping online. It is a freaking nuisance.

"Hey, Milo," Zach interrupted. "I've been meaning to ask you something."

"Shoot," Milo said, taking one of the muffins. I was already on my second, if you're curious.

"I was just wondering," Zach said with studied casualness, "what it was you and Tex were arguing about on Monday in the weight room."

Milo's hand froze with the muffin halfway to his mouth. I stared at Zach, whose eyes were fixed on Milo.

Milo carefully put the muffin down. "I didn't

know there was anyone else there," he said slowly.

"I was nearby," Zach said. "I have pretty good hearing. But I didn't catch what it was about."

Milo was avoiding my eyes. On the one hand, if what Zach had said was true—and it sure seemed to be—then he might have just given me an important clue. On the other hand, Milo now looked really sad and uncomfortable, and it kind of made me want to slug Zach in the nose. I sidled closer to Milo and let my arm brush against his in a sympathetic way. Maybe also in an *Oooh, your arms are sexy* way.

"It was nothing," Milo said with a shrug. He gave me a half smile and touched my free hand lightly. "Just a stupid fight. I feel bad about it now."

"It didn't sound like nothing," Zach pressed. "Didn't I hear you say something about that creepy senior?"

My ears perked up. "Creepy senior?"

"The one who never talks to anyone," Zach said. "He's always taking pictures or scribbling in that notebook. What's his name, Milo?"

"Rowan something," Milo said. "Rowan Cantor, I think. Yeah, it was about him."

Now my senses were on full alert. "Tex and Rowan knew each other?"

"Barely," Milo said, wincing. "That was part of the problem." He sighed. "Tex decided that it was his job as captain to recruit new members of the basketball team, since they lost so badly last year. He noticed that Rowan was tall, which was good enough for him."

"I thought Tex was all about football," I said.

"He did any sport he could fit into his schedule," Milo said. "Basketball, too."

"I can't really picture Rowan playing basketball," I said.

"Exactly," Milo agreed. "I mean, I don't really know the guy, but as far as I can tell, he just wants to be left alone."

"Is that what you were arguing about?" Zach interjected nosily.

"Sort of." Milo rubbed his head. "I thought Tex was kind of harassing him. Like, getting really into his space, you know? Guys on the swim team told me that Tex would throw basketballs at Rowan during gym class and follow him down the hall, badgering him about how the team needed him and stuff. I figured I knew Tex well enough to tell him I thought he should step off. He thought otherwise. He kept saying he thought Rowan was finally getting interested." He glanced at me. "How terrible is that, fighting with a guy the day before he dies? I didn't want to say anything because it's not like I thought Tex was a bad guy. He was just . . . overly enthusiastic, sometimes."

"Sure," I said, nodding. A million things were going through my head. Clicking things. Probably not the things Zach was hoping were going through my head, though.

"You know what we could do?" Milo said to me hopefully, clearly trying to change the subject. "There's this park not far from here that has an amazing hiking trail—the leaves are starting to change and it's not too strenuous and the views are great. Or . . . um . . . do we hate hiking, too?"

Zach snorted. "You'd have better luck getting her to a football game." There was a note of bitterness there; I'd skipped most of Zach's football games when we were dating. I know—it was bad of me. I wanted to be a supportive girlfriend, but (a) boring, (b) cold, (c) confusing, and (d) *mad crazy boring*.

"Hey, shut up," I said. "I can hike. I'd love to go hiking."

"Really?" Milo brightened.

Well, no. Not usually. But for Milo, I was willing to make an exception, even if it meant a truckload of vampire sunscreen and a migraine for the next three days.

"I'll go change," I said. Zach was full-on glaring at me now. I didn't particularly want to leave him alone with Milo. "How about you wait for me in the car?" I said sweetly.

"Okay," he said, his eyes shifting to Zach, so I knew he had the same thought.

"Take some of the muffins," I said as I headed out of the kitchen. "I'll need as many chocolate chips as possible to get me up a hiking trail."

I've always hated putting on sunscreen, but it's a lot more motivating when you imagine bursting into flames than it is when all you have to worry about is maybe skin cancer someday. Yeah, Olympia says the fire thing won't happen, but I've seen too many *Buffy* episodes to feel one hundred percent safe out there. So I slathered the smelly stuff all over my face and arms and hands before putting on khaki cargo pants, an indigo blue T-shirt, and a light blue hoodie.

Zach was standing at the front door when I got downstairs, his arms folded and a deep frown on his face. "So, are you, like, dating that guy or what?" he demanded.

"It's none of your business if I am," I said. "Tell Olympia where I went and that I'll be home in a few hours."

"I can't believe you're going hiking with him," Zach growled. "You never did anything outdoors during the day with me . . . back when I could, I mean."

"Chill out, Zach," I said. "He's part of my murder investigation, all right? Go back to sleep." I pushed past him and ran out to the car, where Milo was waiting for me in his way-too-cute sunglasses.

Despite what I'd said to Zach, as Milo and I climbed the trail I didn't bring up Tex or the murder. Bright orange and gold leaves whirled around us, and the wind tugged at my hair. Halfway along, Milo took my hand to help me over a fallen tree and then didn't let go. It was sweet and comfortable, walking with him like that, with sunshine sparkling down through the trees. It was really easy to forget for a while that I was a vampire. Oh, and that maybe he was, too, only with slightly more murderous tendencies than me.

But I hadn't had any blood that morning—hello, cute boy in my kitchen! Plus it totally doesn't go with banana muffins. So I was feeling sort of faint by the time we got to the top ridge. The bright sunshine up there didn't help either. I sat down on a large boulder in the biggest patch of shade I could find.

"You okay?" Milo asked, handing me a bottle of water.

"Yeah, I'm fine," I said. I tried to give him a reassuring smile. "You're right, it's really pretty up here."

He sat down next to me and put his arm around me. I leaned my head on his shoulder.

The trees rustled overhead, and a star-shaped red leaf drifted down to land on my knee.

"This is kind of weird for me," he said after a long moment.

"What is?"

"Being with a girl." He touched my hair gently. "Falling for someone, I mean, just like that." He chuckled. "I'm not very good at playing it cool, am I?"

"I prefer it that way," I said, tilting my head to look up at him. "I figure, if you like someone, you should—"

And then he kissed me.

Chapter 17

If it turns out that heaven is getting to relive the best moment of your life over and over again, that kiss with Milo is currently my top pick. I mean, not that I'm likely to get *there* anytime soon, being the undead and all.

I didn't want to go home. I wanted to be a normal girl and spend the rest of the day with Milo. I wanted to go to the movies and out to dinner, and then cuddle (or, you know . . . something along those lines) in his car at the end of the night.

But I couldn't. I had to go home, drink my daily recommended dosage of cold animal blood, and then lie in the dark for hours recovering from too much sunshine. Oh, and I also had to solve a murder in the next two days so that my dad wouldn't lock me in a coffin for the next three hundred years. Literally.

My head was pounding by the time Milo dropped me off. I drank two glasses of blood and went straight up to my room, turned off all the lights, and crawled under the covers.

"Serves you right," said a voice from the doorway.

"Go stake yourself," I said, keeping the pillow over my head.

"I don't know what you see in that guy," Zach grumbled.

"Yeah," I said. "Funny, smart, sexy, good-looking, sweet, and a baker. Nothing appealing about that at all."

"But maybe a murderer, right?" Zach said. "That's why you're really dating him, isn't it?"

"I've decided he's not a murderer," I said, peeking out from under the pillow. The light from the hallway spilled into my room around Zach's beefy shape, and I had to cover my eyes again.

"Oh, really?" Zach said. "What brought you to that conclusion all of a sudden?"

Well, for one thing, I highly doubt a murderer could

be that good a kisser. "I've decided it's someone else," I said.

"Yeah? Who?"

I sighed. "That Rowan guy you were talking about. There are too many clues pointing in his direction. Plus he's freaky." *And NOT a good kisser.*

Zach let out a sharp, barking laugh. "Wow," he said. "You really are dumb."

I wriggled deeper into the covers. "I do not have the energy for you right now, Zach."

"Well, I know something you don't know," he said. "And I think maybe you should."

"I've got a good idea," I said. "Why don't you just tell me, instead of acting like a six-year-old? Or else go away and let me sleep."

"There's a reason we're here," Zach said. "In this town, I mean, here and now. I heard Olympia and Wilhelm talking about it. It's because of you."

I shoved the covers back and sat up. Immediately a five-siren alarm went off in my head, like a jackhammer trying to blast through my skull. I clutched my head and tried to glare at Zach.

"What are you talking about?"

"You don't know anything, do you?" he said in that snide way of his. "You don't even know how you really died."

I stopped breathing. Admittedly, this wasn't a huge problem, since I was dead and didn't actually need to. But still, without meaning to, I literally stopped breathing.

"I died in a car accident," I said. "Everyone knows that."

"That's not the whole story," he said. His face was backlit so I couldn't see his expression, but I could practically feel the waves of smugness coming off him. "But you don't know the truth. That's why you have so many issues."

"I do *not* have *issues*," I snapped.

"Olympia and Wilhelm think you do," Zach pointed out. "They think the fact that you turned me is a sign that you still have a lot of your own death issues to work through. That's why they brought you here. Now Wilhelm thinks you killed Tex, and maybe you need to work out your issues inside a padded coffin for a while. I, for one, think he might be right."

I got out of bed, forced myself over to Zach

through the blinding pain, and shoved him out the door so hard he flew across the hall and crashed into the linen closet.

"Hey!" he shouted, staggering to his feet. "I'm just telling the truth; you don't have to be such a—"

I slammed the door in his face. And locked it, and stacked my heaviest pieces of furniture in front of it.

He didn't know what he was talking about. He was just trying to mess with my head.

I should ignore him . . . right?

I sat down at my desk and turned on my computer.

I died about a year and a half ago. It's true that I don't actually remember it. I know—how lame is that? It's like forgetting the name of your first boyfriend, or your own birthday. Those things, I remember. I remember Jeremy Cabot kissing me in the library when we were thirteen. I remember that I accidentally knocked a stack of books onto his feet and broke one of his toes, and that we didn't talk to each other again for a year after that. I remember kissing him again at my fifteenth birthday party, in the closet in my

203

parents' basement. The walls smelled like cedar; his lips tasted like chocolate cupcakes. I remember thinking a year later that maybe we'd be those rare high school sweethearts who really grow up and marry each other.

I'll never see Jeremy again. He thinks I'm dead. He went to my funeral. Olympia saw him there; she says he couldn't stop crying. She said he looked very handsome in a suit.

Olympia watched the funeral from a distance, waiting to collect me later when I woke up in my grave.

That I remember. I still have nightmares about it. I hear vampires are supposed to feel comfortable in confined spaces (like, say, coffins), but it freaked me out like nobody's business when I woke up in the dark with only an inch of space around me on either side.

Or maybe what really traumatized me was realizing that Mom had decided to bury me in this hideous white ruffled dress I once had to wear as a junior bridesmaid. I *hated* that dress, and she knew it. Plus I wonder how the bride (my second cousin, Nicola) felt about that—although she lives in Canada, so maybe she didn't even come to the funeral. Maybe she didn't even know that the dress she picked out so carefully for her special day was now moldering along with me, six feet under.

I really wish my mom had buried me in my favorite jeans and sneakers, maybe with one of my T-shirts ironically advertising a band that doesn't exist. For one thing, it would have been *much* easier to bust out of a coffin in something like that. I practically had to rip off the dress just to move. Thank God only Olympia was waiting for me when I climbed out. You know that dream you have where you're suddenly a vampire and you have to dig your way out of your own grave—oh, and also, you're naked?

Okay, possibly that's just me.

It also would have been nice to have some clothes from my former life that I actually wanted to take with me into my new un-life. Do you know how hard it is to find the perfect jeans? I was half tempted to sneak into my house and steal my favorite pair before we left town, but Olympia put her foot down. Vampires are strictly forbidden to risk any interaction with our living families. If Mom had caught me there, or if she'd noticed the jeans were missing—well, I don't know what would have happened, but Olympia made it sound awfully dire. Something about hosts of bloodthirsty vampire hunters coming after all of us, which sounds like kind of an overreaction to a pair of stolen jeans, if you ask me.

I think perhaps she's making up the vampire hunter story, but I can see that it would have been a pretty awkward conversation if Mom did walk in. "Um . . . I am the ghoooooost of your dauuuuuuuughter! My spirit haunts the earthly realm! I shall never be at peace . . . unless I have these jeans. Don't ask questions! Toodle-oooooooooooo." Hurl myself out the window, et cetera.

So, the point is, rebuilding your wardrobe from scratch is just one of the many un-fun things about becoming a vampire. Especially in our family, since Olympia is fairly keen on avoiding lawbreaking of any sort—such as, say, using one's vampire strength to rip off the doors of a mall late at night, when mirrors don't matter, and rampaging through the nearest Old Navy. Doesn't that sound awesome? I told her that might help make up for the being-a-vampire bit, but all I got back is that it would also attract "unwanted attention." For someone who's already lived, like, seven hundred years, Olympia is not very adventurous.

Here's what I do remember about the night I died.

Mom and I were fighting, as usual. *No, you can't get your belly button pierced. No, you can't go camping with Jeremy. No, you can't stay out one second past your curfew.* I'd finally dragged Dad into the argument, and he said he thought it would be fine if I went to this *one* party, as long as he drove me and Jeremy (neither of us had our licenses yet) and I came home on time.

I was like, *OMG, so embarrassing*, but on the other hand, convenient. I didn't really want to get a ride from one of the senior girls, who were always flirting with Jeremy, or the senior boys, who drove like lunatics anyway.

And then it turned out the party was only a few blocks away, so perhaps I could have skipped the indignity of the parental ride after all. Of course, as we got out of the car, Dad said, "All right, hon, you give me a call and I'll come get you whenever you're ready."

"Okay," I said, rolling my eyes. "Thanks, Dad."

That was my last conversation with him.

The party is kind of a blur. Not because I drank; I've always hated the taste of beer. Mostly Jeremy and I used parties like that as an excuse to dance with each other a lot and then find a dark corner for smooching as long as we could. Yeah, we were one of *those* couples, the kind everyone else veers around all night.

I don't remember much about that particular party, except that I think Jeremy wasn't feeling well. So I think we decided to leave early . . . but I'm not sure when we left, or whose car I got into.

The next thing I *do* remember is lying in the road and thinking, *Why am I in the road? This doesn't seem like a very safe place to lie down.* I got the impression I was on a quiet suburban street, with hardly any traffic and dim, distantly spaced streetlights barely competing with the moon. I couldn't move my head to look around; I didn't know if there was anyone else near me. And then I felt a wild spasm of pain in my head and my legs, and I realized that there was blood all over me and under me and all around me.

And *I couldn't move.*

Oh, I thought. *I'm dying. That is really not okay with me.* The rest of my brain rejected the whole idea. *No, someone will come for you. Someone is coming to help. Just hang on . . . someone will be here soon.*

Minutes ticked away as I felt fainter and fainter and the pain grew worse. *There must have been a crash,* I thought fuzzily. *I must have been thrown out of the car. So where's the car? Where are the other people in the car?* I blinked up at the stars. *Who was I with? Who am I waiting for? I'm waiting for someone. Someone specific. Someone has gone to bring help.*

And then they came.

They came to save me, but not quite in the way I'd been hoping for.

Olympia and Wilhelm. Bert and Crystal. They must have smelled the blood. They hadn't added anyone to their family in a long time. I could hear them arguing about me as they got closer, although I had no idea what any of it meant.

My head was really fuzzy by the time they arrived, so it didn't seem odd to me that pale people with fangs were suddenly holding my hands and brushing back my hair.

"Do you want to die?" Olympia whispered.

I'm not sure if I actually spoke, but she could see the *no* in my eyes.

"You don't have to . . . not exactly. We can save you. You can be one of us," she said. "But it won't be the same. You have to understand."

"Just do it," Wilhelm snapped. "We don't have time to mollycoddle her about it."

Bert and Crystal nodded. The moonlight reflected off Bert's glasses, making his face blank and inscrutable. My first, silvery impression of Crystal was of long fangs and orange tie-dye and an expression that was compassionate and hungry at the same time.

"She has to agree," Olympia said. Her long, dark hair hung down, brushing against my face. "That's our rule."

This time I did speak. Somehow I found enough breath to whisper, "Yes."

Olympia bent down toward my neck. Crystal took my wrist in her small, pale hands. Tiny explosions of pain in both places, and then a weird rush of ecstasy, and then Bert's voice saying, "You'll die for a little while. We'll be there when you wake up. Don't be afraid."

And then blackness.

Of course it was a car accident. It must have been. Whoever was driving had hit something—or been hit—and I'd been thrown out of the car. What I didn't know was what had happened to everyone else. As soon as I crawled out of my grave, I asked Olympia if Jeremy was all right.

"He is fine," she said. "Nobody else was hurt in the accident."

There, you see? Accident. I remembered those words exactly. That was all I wanted to know about my own death. I figured if I tried to find out more, it would only make me miss my old life. Plus, talk about depressing.

But now I sat at my computer, took a deep breath, and typed *Phoebe Tanaka* into Google.

I don't recommend this—Googling yourself, I mean. I especially don't recommend it if you're dead, and if reading mournful memorial tributes to yourself will make you cry for hours, and if then discovering that there aren't nearly as many mournful memorial tributes as you were hoping for will make you disgruntled and cranky.

But I did find out what happened to me, thanks to all the news articles.

LOCAL GIRL KILLED IN HIT AND RUN

POLICE SAY DYING TEEN COULD HAVE BEEN SAVED

NO TRACE OF HIT-AND-RUN KILLER

QUESTIONS LINGER IN TEEN'S DEATH

There were interviews with Jeremy's parents; they wouldn't let the reporters near him, though, because some of them were sniffing for more scandal—like maybe Jeremy was the one who'd killed me. Mr. Cabot told the police that Jeremy had gotten a ride and I had decided to walk home from the party. It was only nine thirty at night, after all. It wasn't far. I'd be home in no time; no need to bother my dad.

And then a car had come out of the night, as I walked along those quiet suburban streets, and hit me.

"She could have lived," said the doctor interviewed for the article. "If the driver had stopped and called for help—she'd still be alive today."

But by the time someone finally found me, it was too late.

My hands were so numb, I could hardly move the mouse. I clicked on the photo that went with the article, blowing it up to fill the screen. It was a shot of my funeral. There were Mom and Dad and Apolla, standing close to the grave and crying. More people were there than I'd have expected . . . classmates, teachers, relatives . . .

As I scanned the crowd around the hole in the ground, a face jumped out at me.

I leaned forward, wiping away my tears, and peered at it more closely.

I felt like I'd been punched in the stomach. I knew that face. But it didn't make any sense.

Rowan Cantor was at my funeral.

Chapter 18

𝓘 decided I was well within my rights to skip school on Monday. It isn't every day that you experience horrifying revelations about your own death, after all. It seemed like the perfect time to spend an entire day in bed, sleeping off my sun headache and trying not to think about what I was going to say when I saw Rowan again.

By the time I woke up Monday night, I wasn't sad anymore. I was angry. Like, seriously, wholeheartedly furious.

"Where are you going?" Olympia called from the den as I marched into the kitchen.

"To take care of my *issues*," I called back.

She appeared in the doorway with a concerned look as I choked down a glass of blood.

I didn't plan to get faint during this encounter, no, sir.

"What does that mean?" she asked.

I put the glass in the sink and stormed out the door without answering her.

Her expression was nothing compared to the look on Albert Cantor's face when he opened the door and found out it was me pounding on the other side. He went pale and sweaty and looked freaked out, as if he was facing a ghost— which, I realized, he basically was.

I didn't say anything to him. I needed answers from Rowan. I went right past him and down the hall into Rowan's room.

Rowan was lying on his mattress with one pale arm flung across his eyes. He sat up, blinking, as I slammed the door behind me.

"You lied to me," I said. That was not the most terrible thing he'd done, but it seemed like a good place to start.

"What?" He rubbed his face and squinted at me.

I tugged the page I'd printed out of my pocket and dropped it on the mattress beside him. "You didn't move here from San Francisco."

All the blood seemed to drain out of his face as he stared at the photograph.

"I was just—" he stammered, climbing to his feet. "No, we just happened to be—"

"Don't *lie* to me!" I yelled. I crossed the room and pulled his locked metal box out of his desk. Before he could move, I ripped the top off, breaking the lock and the hinges. Most of the papers inside were articles about my death. I'd expected that, but it was still kind of a shock to see proof. I grabbed the papers and turned around, brandishing them at him. "It was you, wasn't it? *You're* the driver who killed Phoebe."

Rowan's shocked, terrified eyes met mine, and suddenly a memory came flooding back: of those same eyes looking down at me, framed by moonlight and bright headlights.

"You said you'd get help," I said, pointing at him. "You said you'd come back to save her. Instead you let her bleed to death all alone in the middle of the road." *Alone until the vampires came, anyway.*

Rowan reached out his arms like he was looking for something to hold him up. Finding nothing, he fell to his knees in front of me. "How—how do you know that?" he croaked in terror.

"Is that why you're so keen to talk about death all the time?" I asked. "Because you're a killer?"

"It was an accident," he whispered. "I didn't see her."

"But you just left her there," I said. "You drove away."

"There was so much blood." He clawed at his face like he was trying to rip the memories out of his head. "I thought she would die before I got back. I was scared—I was scared—I was so scared—"

"*You* were scared?" I said. "How do you think *she* felt?"

"Oh, God," Rowan said in a horrible, wretched voice.

I'll admit it. I kind of wanted to bite him. Or rather, I kind of wanted to kill him, and *then* bite him, because I definitely didn't want creepy vampire Rowan hanging around in addition to lecherous vampire Zach. I wanted him gone.

But that wouldn't solve any of my problems, most especially the one where Wilhelm and Olympia thought I was the murdering type.

"You're going to confess," I said, grabbing Rowan's T-shirt and yanking him to his feet. I didn't care if my strength startled him. "You're going to turn yourself in so they know what happened. Jeremy and"—I'd nearly said *Mom and Dad*—"everyone else."

"No," Rowan said, struggling. He tried to pry my hands off his shirt, but he couldn't. "I can't. I won't. Dad won't let me anyway. Besides it was two years ago—it's over now—"

"It's not over for some people," I said, taking a step toward the door.

Rowan started flailing. He threw a punch at my face, which I dodged, and then tried to knock me down with a sudden lunge. I flipped him over so he landed on his back with a thud. With a yelp of anger, he seized my foot and jerked hard. I caught myself on my hands as I fell and pushed myself back up, then kicked his hands aside and planted my boot firmly in the middle of his chest.

Have I mentioned there are *some* benefits to being a vampire?

"You didn't have anything to do with Tex, did you?" I asked.

"Of course not!" he cried. "Dad won't even let me out of the house after dark anymore." He rolled suddenly sideways, jumped to his feet, and tackled me. I threw him over my head and he smashed into the opposite wall.

"It's not going to be so easy to kill me this time," I said.

Rowan's blue eyes went wide. "It *is* you," he whispered. He dove for his desk drawer, grabbed something out of it, and spun around to point it at me.

A gun, small and black and gleaming.

"Are you kidding?" I said, putting my hands on my hips.

"I will shoot you," he said.

"That," I said, "would make me *really* mad."

"Go away," he said. "Stop haunting me. Leave me alone!"

"You need help, Rowan," I said, taking a step toward him. "Look at this house. Look at this room. Look at *you*, and your *incredibly creepy* corpse photos. Your guilt is destroying your whole life, and either you need to deal with it, or you need to be locked up so it doesn't explode into something like, say, shooting a girl in your bedroom."

Oh, I thought at the same time, *I guess that's kind of what Wilhelm and Olympia were going for, too.* It all made sense to me now. They'd known about Rowan; they'd brought me here and even pointed him out expressly to make sure I confronted my old demons so I could move on and become a well-integrated member of vampire society. Or something like that.

Well, they didn't have to be so *vague* and *mysterious* about it. They really could have saved me a lot of time by just telling me a few things, since I didn't even know I *had* death issues to deal with in the first place.

The bedroom door behind me suddenly flew open. Startled, Rowan jumped and the gun went off.

"Rowan!" his dad shouted in terror.

But I had jumped at the same time, knocking the gun aside, so the bullet thumped harmlessly into the closet door. I yanked the gun out of his hand and threw it at Albert. He caught it with both hands and held it as if he'd never seen anything like it before.

"You need to deal with this," I said to him. I pointed at Rowan, who was sliding slowly down to the floor. "You can't keep lying and hiding and hoping that if you run it'll never catch up with you."

"What did he tell you?" Albert said weakly.

"She knows, Dad," Rowan said. "About that girl."

"Phoebe," I said, still angry. "Her name was Phoebe."

Rowan stared at me, all the fight drained out of him. "It's you, isn't it?" he whispered.

"Don't talk crazy, son," Albert said. He looked exhausted. "She's right. We can't live like this anymore. You're losing your mind, and I feel like I am, too."

"I'll be checking the papers for news of your confession," I said, stepping over the piles of clothes as I headed to the door. "Don't run again, or I'll find you."

I left them like that, facing each other across Rowan's tiny room. My killer and his dad, who had covered it up and helped him run.

I didn't know if his confession would make my parents feel any better, but it was the best resolution I could give them from where I was now.

So take that, death issues.

Chapter 19

$\mathcal{I}$ thought about going home and getting back into bed, but honestly, there was only one person I wanted to see right then. And I *needed* to see him, too, for a few reasons. Not all of which involved kissing.

Because if Tex's vampire murderer wasn't Rowan, then I had a bad feeling it had to be Milo.

Sure, Daniel was acting pretty suspicious with the way he kept nosing around the crime. But there was no evidence linking him to Tex—no sign that they knew each other, no particularly vampire-like behavior I could point to. I got the feeling Daniel really was trying to solve the murder, for whatever reasons of his own.

So that left Milo. The red bead, the fight in the gym, the fact that they could easily have been in the locker room, near the mirrors, at the same time. I had to find out for sure.

All the way over to his house, I tried coming up with explanations that would make killing Tex okay. Maybe it was an accident. Maybe Tex killed himself, and Milo just happened to wander by and bite him. Maybe Tex attacked him, and Milo had to throw him out a window in self-defense. It was possible . . . right?

I really didn't want him to face some kind of vampire punishment. It would be awfully hard to keep dating him if he was locked up in a padded coffin, for instance. And I did want to keep dating him, so long as he could explain Tex's death. Dating a vampire might be tough, but I didn't think it could be any tougher than trying to date a human.

I found his house with no trouble: small but friendly-looking, with dark blue shutters against the white wood. It was nearly eleven o'clock at night, and all the lights downstairs were off. Only two of the upstairs windows had lights glowing behind the blinds, including the one Milo had said was his room.

Well, I wasn't exactly planning on ringing

the doorbell anyway. And Milo's house had a tall oak tree growing outside his window, unlike the dastardly army of prickly hemlocks at Tex's.

I checked to make sure the street was empty and then launched myself up the tree, leaping to the first branch and then climbing hand over hand until I was level with Milo's window. I lowered myself carefully onto the roof below his window and peeked inside.

The first thing I saw was books. Tall book-shelves lined the opposite side of the room, reaching from the wall to the door and the floor to the ceiling. Milo's bed, covered in a dark blue comforter, was on this side of the room, near the window seat that was right below me. On the wall to my left, under another window, was his desk, which was also covered in books, half of them lying open next to his computer. On the wall to my right were his closet and a chest of drawers. His clothes were neatly put away, and there was none of the mess I'd seen in Tex's and Rowan's rooms. The wall-to-wall carpet was a soft dove-gray, and the walls were a warm orangey-peach.

Best news of all? No mirrors.

Milo was nowhere to be seen; the room was empty. There was a screen covering the open window, but it was easy to swing it aside so I could slip through. I replaced it carefully behind me as I climbed onto the window seat and sat down to wait for him.

Music was playing quietly from the computer speakers; I recognized a OneRepublic song before it faded into Regina Spektor. Well, I certainly approved of that. Also of his screensaver, which was a nice, tasteful aquarium full of swimming fish instead of Angelina Jolie. I realized there was also a real aquarium tucked in among the bookshelves. Tiny, glowing purple and blue and yellow fish floated dreamily among the bubbles.

I noticed a trunk at my feet, to the right of the window seat. It looked old and weathered, as if it had been around the world a few times. The lid was slightly ajar, propped up on something that stuck out on one side. I squinted at it, trying to figure out what it was. It looked like the end of a crossbow.

A crossbow?

227

Curious, I nudged the trunk open a little further with my foot. I caught a glimpse of a pile of pale wood, but before I could nose around any further, the bedroom door opened. I jerked my foot away from the trunk in a hurry, but Milo didn't notice, because he had a towel over his head.

I draped myself casually (and, I hoped, alluringly) across the window seat as he finished drying his hair. Just like at our first meeting, he was shirtless and barefoot, wearing only a pair of khaki shorts. And he had on his cute-cute glasses. He had clearly just gotten out of the shower.

Milo emerged from under the towel and turned to hang it on the back of his door. When he spotted me out of the corner of his eye, he jumped about a foot, letting out a shout of surprise.

"Shhh," I said, putting one finger to my lips.

"Milo?" I heard a male voice call from down the hall. "Is everything okay?"

"Yeah, Dad," Milo called back. "Sorry, just startled myself." He smiled at me. "Wow, you took me kind of literally, didn't you?" he said softly.

I gave him an innocent expression. "I thought I was supposed to come in this way."

"Oh, yeah," he said. "Doors are so overrated." He came closer and peered out the window behind me. "Did you really climb that tree?"

"I'm pretty agile," I said with a wink. A wink that I hoped would convey, *So since we're both vampires, let's just admit it and get on with the sexy vampire dating.*

Although, I reminded myself, *I should probably deal with the whole murder thing first.*

"I missed you in school today," he said.

"I missed you, too," I said, taking his hands. "I wanted to talk to you about something."

He pulled me to my feet and kissed me. All thoughts of dead football players flew out of my head. He must have killed Tex by accident. Someone who kissed like Milo couldn't possibly be a coldhearted killer. The computer was playing Jack Johnson's "Better Together," and I just wanted to stay inside Milo's arms for the rest of eternity.

I trailed my fingers up his chest to his neck

and buried them in his hair. He pulled me closer, kissing me deeper. The symbol on his necklace swung forward and bumped my bare skin, just below my wrist.

A sharp pain shot up my arm to my shoulder. I jerked back, startled, and at the same time he moved to pull me away from the window, so we sort of stumbled sideways. He accidentally jostled the mouse on his desk, and the fish screensaver disappeared.

The image that flashed up in its place was a split screen of two photos. One of them was, unmistakably, a close-up of the bite marks on Tex's neck. The other was similar, but this neck was thicker and the hair near it was long and dark instead of short and blond like Tex's. I noticed right away that the bite marks were smaller and cleaner, as well—a tinier set of teeth were involved, although still definitely a vampire's.

Little electronic Post-It notes dotted the screen. I saw that one was labeled *RC* and another *DM*, but I didn't catch what any of them said before Milo jumped in the way of the screen and quickly clicked it closed.

I was staring at him, openmouthed, when he finally turned back to face me. His expression was nervous and sheepish.

"Um," he said. "I have something to tell you, too."

Chapter 20

Milo gently led me over to the bed and we both sat down, facing each other.

"This is going to be hard for you to believe," he said, taking a deep breath.

"Try me," I said. *You're a vampire? It's okay, so am I! Problem solved, let's hook up!*

Except I was starting to get nervous. The images on the screen . . . the crossbow in the trunk . . . the vial of clear liquid sitting on his bedside table, which suddenly caught my attention, due to the shiny cross on its side.

Had those been *stakes* inside the trunk? What kind of vampire would keep stakes lying around? Certainly not me. I would definitely trip over something and accidentally impale myself if I had a stake anywhere near my bedroom.

"The first thing you have to know," he said,

"is that vampires are real."

You don't say. Some instinct stopped me from saying, "Yeah, duh. I am one." Instead I just looked at him. He read my expression as disbelief.

"I know, it sounds crazy," he said. "But it's true. There are vampires, and they live out in regular society, just like you and me."

Yes. Well, just like me, anyway.

I nodded at the computer. "So those photos . . . ?"

"Those were vampire attacks," Milo said. "One of them was Tex Harrison. The other was the corpse I told you about—the guy in the alley a few years ago. I'm afraid I didn't tell you everything, Kira. That guy was actually the reason my dad and I moved here."

A shiver ran down my spine. I didn't think I liked where this was going. "The reason?" I said faintly.

"Kira," Milo said, touching my face. His brown eyes were serious behind his glasses. "My dad and I—we're vampire hunters."

There was perfect silence for a moment. Even the music had stopped. It was like the universe froze, the way I wanted to freeze, here in this moment before everything unraveled.

Then I heard something *pitter-patter* against the windowpane. It was starting to rain.

"Say something." Milo pressed my hand. "You look so pale."

I shook my head. "There's no such thing," I said, hardly knowing what I was saying.

"Vampires are real, Kira," Milo said earnestly, misunderstanding me. "There's one in our school. He killed Tex, and he'll probably kill again. I've been trying to catch him, but it's complicated."

TELL ME ABOUT IT.

He rubbed his free hand across his forehead. "We don't know if it's the same person who killed the guy in the alley. We've been trying to catch that vampire since we moved here. But the bite marks are different, so I think it's someone new. Which means there's more than one vampire in this town."

Um, yes. At least six that I know of, plus whoever killed Tex.

"What, um—" My voice wavered; I had to clear my throat and start again. "What would

234

you do if you caught them?" I hoped I sounded more curious than, you know, absolutely terrified.

"What vampire hunters do," Milo said. He had both my hands in his now and was rubbing his thumbs reassuringly across my knuckles. His hands were really warm. That probably should have tipped me off sooner, I realized, but I hadn't wanted to believe that he was human.

And I certainly hadn't wanted to know that his mission in life was to kill folks like me.

"You'd stake them?" I squeaked.

Milo looked down at my hands. "There are a few other ways, too," he said.

"So you've . . . done that before?"

"I haven't," Milo said, avoiding my eyes. "I'm still in training. But my dad has. He's been doing this a long time, and so did his mom and dad before him." He finally looked up and saw the expression on my face. He ran his hands up my arms to my shoulders. "Kira, it's okay, don't look so scared. Vampires are like sharks—they kill people much less frequently than you would think. You're perfectly safe, especially as long as you're with me. I'll protect you." He gave me a lopsided grin. "You should see me with a cross-bow. I wish I got to use it more often; I think it'd be a real hit with the ladies."

Yeah, maybe not so much with the fanged ladies, though.

"Anyway," he said. "I wanted to tell you. Even before you saw my investigation notes." He tilted his head toward the computer. "I wanted to be honest with you."

"I just—had no idea," I said, trying to stop my voice from shaking. "You seem so, um . . . normal."

"I am normal," Milo said, "most of the time. Although I have to admit that's one of the things I like most about being with you—that it makes me feel like a regular guy, living a normal life and dating a really hot girl."

I let out a snort of laughter, which he misin-terpreted. "Yeah, okay," he said. "I guess maybe it isn't so normal to date a girl as beautiful as you. I got lucky." He cupped his hands around my face.

Oh, why did he have to be so perfect in every other way?

I leaned forward and touched his lips gently

236

with mine. He kissed me, softly at first, and then more passionately, wrapping my hair around his hands as we clutched each other closer.

"Wait," I said, breaking free for a moment. "Is—is that a vampire hunter thing?" I pointed to the necklace and the strange symbol on it.

"Yeah," Milo said. He touched it with two fingers. "It belonged to my mom. The symbol is supposed to be a protection against vampires."

What if you don't want to be protected? Hypothetically speaking?

"Oh," I said aloud, remembering the sharp pain it had given me. "I thought maybe it was . . . it kind of freaks me out."

"No worries," Milo said with a smile. He unclasped it and dropped it on his bedside table. I wondered what his dad would think about that. Poor Milo—he wanted to be a badass vampire hunter, but really he was sweet and trusting and just had no idea how much trouble he could get into. "Better?" Milo asked.

"Much," I said, and pulled him to me again.

Somehow we found ourselves lying down on the bed, kissing and running our hands over each other. *His arms are perfect,* I thought, feeling his muscles under my fingers. *His shoulders are perfect. His neck is perfect.*

This was nothing like Zach. This was a million times more exciting and wonderful than being with Zach.

Which was a bad thing. I thought I had myself under control after Zach, but with him I was only hungry. Now I was falling head over heels for Milo, and I wanted him so badly, and his heartbeat was pulsing so fast and so close and so alive. . . . His smooth brown skin was right in front of me as he kissed his way down my face to my neck. I could feel his heart beating faster and my own control weakening. I wanted to bite him. I wanted to sink my teeth in and take us both over the edge.

I could feel my teeth starting to move. Milo's hands were at my waist.

What was I doing?

If Milo knew what I was . . . if he knew the real me . . . he would stake me right away. Or set me on fire, or do something else too horrible to contemplate. And then he'd remember who I lived with, and all of them—Olympia, Wilhelm,

Zach, Bert, and Crystal—would be dust before sunrise. Unless they defended themselves, in which case it was Milo who would be dead.

Daniel had said I was playing a dangerous game.

No, *this* was a dangerous game. A deadly game.

I shoved Milo off of me with more force than I intended. He went right over the side of the bed and hit the floor with a thump.

"I'm sorry," I said, scrambling to my feet. "I'm sorry, I can't."

"It's okay, it's okay," Milo said. He pushed himself up and held his hand out to me, the smile already coming back. "I'm sorry, I didn't mean to—you're just so—"

I stepped away from him, back toward the window. I felt hollow and frightened of what had nearly happened. "I mean, I really can't," I said. I climbed onto the window seat. "I'm sorry, Milo."

His face fell. "Wait, Kira, don't go. Is it what I told you? It's not so bad, I promise." He caught my hand and looked up at me pleadingly. "It's raining. Please stay. What can I do to make you stay?"

I shook my head, feeling like I was about to cry. "We can't. Goodbye, Milo." I couldn't say anything else. I pushed aside the screen and ducked out the window.

Raindrops splattered against my T-shirt as I swung out on the branch and crawled down the tree. The bark was slick and wet under my hands, and I had to climb carefully. By the time I got down to the ground, I was soaked through.

I looked up and saw Milo watching me out the window, one hand pressed to the screen like he was trying to reach through it and bring me back.

I turned and walked away, letting the rain wash away the tears running down my face.

Chapter 21

It was midnight, and I didn't want to go home. I didn't want to deal with Zach's smugness, and I did not want to discuss my feelings about my "death issues" with Olympia or Crystal, and I most definitely did not want to give Wilhelm an update on my murder investigation, which was supposed to be solved by Wednesday. At least now I had only one suspect left.

So I went to the cemetery. It was actually kind of cool and spooky in the storm, with thunder rumbling and lightning flashing overhead. This particular cemetery is huge, with lots of big, fancy tombstones and crypts and things, but the main reason I like it is that there's never anyone here, at least at night, so I don't have to worry about pretending that I'm a normal girl.

I found a gravestone that was like a big stone

box sticking out of the ground. I lifted myself onto the top of it and lay down on my back, closing my eyes and letting the rain pour over my face. I could feel the crackle and energy of the lightning and the rumble of the thunder shaking the sky. The raindrops pounded into my skin, and I made myself stop breathing so I wouldn't drown, although I'm pretty sure vampires can't drown. I just lay there, as still as the grave I was lying on, trying not to think about Milo or Rowan or mysterious vampire attacks.

A hand touched my face, then moved to my forehead, pushing back my wet hair and feeling for my temperature. I opened my eyes.

Daniel was standing over me, looking concerned. He put his hands on either side of my face and stared into my eyes. Have I mentioned before what great eyes he has? I figured I wouldn't mind just lying there, gazing into them for a while. It was better than moping about Milo, that's for sure.

"Kira," he said, moving his hands to my shoulders. He pulled me up into a sitting position and sat on the stone facing me. His hands felt my arms, and then he took my hands and started rubbing them. "Kira, you're freezing."

"That's okay," I said numbly.

"It's not okay," he said. He glanced around and stood up. With a single graceful movement, he put one arm under my knees and one arm around my back, and lifted me up.

Wow, I thought. *This is kind of cool.* He started walking as if I weighed nothing at all.

"I can walk," I said to him. "I mean, this is thrilling, but kind of unnecessary."

"Shush," Daniel said. "We're having a moment."

"Oh," I said. "Okay." I realized he was heading for a crypt up ahead where we could go inside and get dry. I put my arms around his neck and leaned against his chest. His white shirt was soaking wet, so it didn't matter that it was buttoned up. Casually, I slid one hand to the side of his neck.

Daniel stepped inside the semidarkness of the crypt, which was lined with silky-smooth white marble. No coffins in the middle of the floor here; the denizens of this burial place were neatly stored behind engraved labels on the wall. A green-and-black star pattern was embedded in the marble floor, and a large bronze urn full of flowers stood opposite the door.

The sound of the storm subsided as we moved under the roof. Lightning lit up Daniel's face as he smiled at me.

"That is much better," he said. Just then he noticed where my hand was. He looked at it sideways. "Er—what are you doing?" He set me down on my feet abruptly and stepped back.

"I knew it!" I said. "You have no pulse! I knew it! Well, except for the part where I just figured it out, but it makes sense!" I pushed my wet hair back, wishing I looked a little more commanding and a little less wet. "You're a vampire!"

"So are you!" he said indignantly.

"Yeah," I said, "well, but I'm the good kind. Wait, you knew that?"

"Of course I knew that," he said. "Why do you think I've been watching you?"

"Because I'm irresistible?" I said. "And you're totally falling for me?"

He ducked his head, rubbing the back of his neck. "Well . . . that, too."

"Really?" I said, crossing my arms. "Or have

you just been messing with me?"

"Look," he said, "all right, yes, at first I was just investigating you because I thought you were Tex's murderer, but then once I spent some time with you, I really started to like—"

"What?" I exploded. "No, no, *no!* *I* am investigating *you* because *you're* Tex's murderer! I can't believe you thought it was me!"

"It's not you?" he said.

"It's not *you*?" I said.

Lightning flashed again. We stared at each other.

"It has to be you," I said. "You're a vampire."

"So are you," he said again. "And my family has a strict no-biting rule."

"So does mine!" I protested.

"That's why they sent me to solve the murder," Daniel said, taking a step closer to me. "I could fit in the best, although I haven't attended high school in decades. I'm afraid it hasn't gotten more interesting. Except for you being there, of course."

"Don't go off topic," I said. "Well, okay, you can get a little off-topic. Really? Me?"

He reached toward my face and then dropped his hand again. "You are by far the most interesting thing at that school, Kira," he said. "Not least because of your violent history."

I winced. "If you're talking about Zach, that wasn't my idea."

"We figured that out," Daniel said, "from the newspaper accounts and our private sources. That's why you're still alive. Otherwise one of my family would probably have staked you by now."

"Yikes," I said, with a shudder I tried to hide. "They sound friendly. I can't wait to meet them."

"We have to execute dangerous vampires," Daniel said. "It's the only way to protect the rest of us." He looked down at his hands. "It happened to one of my sisters—she went too far, and if we hadn't stopped her, she would have kept killing. The one death she caused brought too much attention to us as it is." His eyes met mine again. "Some of us think there are vampire hunters in town already, searching for us."

I didn't tell him about Milo. I couldn't. I didn't know what he would do with that information, and even if Milo was on a lifelong mission to exterminate my kind, I still didn't want anything to happen to him.

"Oh?" I said instead.

"That's why we had to solve this murder," Daniel said. "We prefer to deal with such things ourselves."

"Well, it wasn't me," I said. "I don't know why you would think it was. Okay, apart from the whole being-at-the-murder-scene thing. And the breaking-into-Tex's-house thing. But you did all that, too, by the way." I rubbed my arms, feeling cold and wet. "I was just trying to solve the stupid murder. My family thinks I did it, which is, like, totally unfair, by the way, because I so totally did not. I have to figure out who did it by tomorrow, or else I'll be in big trouble. So if it's not you, either, then I'm kind of screwed."

I gave him a hopeful look. "Any chance you've got some helpful clues? You know, that don't point to me?"

Daniel took my hand and drew me closer to him, smoothing back my wet hair with his free hand.

"Kira," he said. "You're not going to like this."

"What?"

"I was near the school when the murder happened," he said softly. "I heard the glass break and the body fall. But by the time I got there, the killer was gone. He must have heard me coming—that's why he didn't finish feeding. Tex's corpse was lying there bleeding and abandoned. But I could smell the fresh blood . . . enough to follow the vampire's trail."

"You followed him?" I asked, tilting my head to look into his eyes.

"I followed the trail," Daniel said, "all the way back to your house."

Chapter 22

"That's impossible," I said. I tried to pull away from him, but he held my hand firmly.

"It's not," he said. "That's why I suspected you. You seemed like the most likely option."

"Well, I *am* the most likely option," I admitted, "but it wasn't me, so it can't have been anyone else in my family, either."

"Are you sure?" he said. "Do you know them so well? Couldn't one of them be hiding a secret?"

"Why would they do that?" I said. "Why would any of them? Zach and Bert were out of town on a blood run, Crystal would never hurt anyone, and my parents are way too smart to leave their evidence lying around. It's totally impossible."

"Give them another look," Daniel said intently.

"See if you can find anything. I want to help you, Kira. I want to go back to my family and tell them that they don't have to worry about this. I want to keep you safe."

It seemed like lots of boys were offering to keep me safe tonight, all while making my life way too complicated and difficult.

I sat down on the marble floor and put my head in my hands. Daniel knelt beside me and rubbed my back gently.

Don't cry, I ordered myself fiercely. *You've had enough crying for one night. For one immortal lifetime, in fact.*

"It'll be all right," Daniel said.

"Easy for you to say," I said. "Are you *sure* it wasn't you?"

"If you'd like to meet my sisters, you can hear my alibi," he said.

I shivered again. "No thanks." I sighed and slid down until I could rest my head in his lap. "I've had kind of a rough night."

He took one of my hands. "Tell me about it."

I wanted to. But I didn't tell him anything about Milo. I told him about Rowan instead,

250

how I'd thought he was the vampire and then found out instead that he was the guy who killed me.

"Good Lord," Daniel said, running his fingers through my hair. "I can see how that would be a little traumatizing."

I closed my eyes. I liked the feeling of his strong, elegant hands. This was what I had wanted—a dashing, handsome vampire to date. But I couldn't stop thinking about Milo. I'd been so comfortable with him. I'd wanted him to know me, and now I knew that would never be possible.

"What about that swimmer?" Daniel asked, almost as if he'd read my mind, but I knew he couldn't do that or he'd have stopped suspecting me long ago. "The one I've seen you with a few times. Are you . . . dating him?"

"No," I said, with a stab of sadness. "I was investigating him, too. But it turns out he's got nothing to do with any of this." Well, at least in the not-being-a-murderer sense. "Wait—were you the one watching us at the pool?"

Daniel nodded. "I thought—I was afraid that

you might be planning to bite him, too."

"If I weren't so tired, I would smack you," I said, poking his knee. "I am not that kind of girl, okay? Evidence to the contrary not-withstanding."

"All right, all right," Daniel said with a small laugh. "Anyway, I'm glad. That you're not dating him, I mean."

I didn't say anything. I closed my eyes again, and despite the fact that it was the middle of the night, I felt myself drifting off to sleep.

The next thing I knew, Daniel was shaking my shoulder. "Kira, wake up," he whispered. "We should get out of the cemetery before the sun's up."

I sat up groggily. I felt clammy and chilled, and my damp clothes still clung to me. I was sure my hair had dried in some outrageously silly way while I'd slept.

"Oh, this is glamorous," I said, flattening my hair. "I'm sorry I fell asleep."

"It's all right," Daniel said. He stood up and helped me to my feet. "I didn't mind." He put his arms around my waist and looked into my eyes. "Everything will be okay, Kira. Maybe I should come over after school, and we can finally solve this."

"No," I said. "I mean—give me a little time. I need to do this myself." I wasn't sure what "this" was, though. Accuse my family members? Invade their privacy to search for clues? Where would I even begin?

I started out of the crypt, but Daniel caught my hand and pulled me back. He kissed me, long and seriously. I'll admit, it made me feel better.

"You see?" he said as he let me go. "I wasn't messing with you. That part was real."

"See you at school," I said, returning his smile as I ducked out the door.

The storm had passed, and the air was really cold and bright and sharp. The sky was lightening slowly from blue to pale orange. Wet grass soaked my sneakers and the hem of my jeans as I ran through the cemetery and swung out the gates toward home.

Was it true? Was it someone in my house? I didn't know what to think about that. If so, was bad enough that he or she had killed Tex, but then to let me take the blame? Without saying a word to defend me? I couldn't believe any of them would do that.

When I came in the back door, Crystal and Bert were at the kitchen counter. Only instead of sitting next to each other and cuddling like they usually do, they were sitting on opposite sides. Crystal was eating her blood-and-cheese omelet in pointed, cranky silence. Bert had his nose buried in the paper and didn't seem to notice.

"Hey, Bert," I said, kicking off my shoes. I hoped neither of them could hear the tension in my voice. "Where did you guys go to get the blood last week? It tastes marginally less gross than usual."

"Lexington," Bert said curtly. He didn't look up from the paper. "It was a long drive."

"Yeah?" I said. "Good thing you had Zach for company."

"He's a strong guy," Bert said. "Very helpful."

"You saw them leave?" I asked Crystal. I

opened the fridge and poured myself a glass of blood, trying to behave like this was any ordinary morning.

"I sure did," Crystal said. She stared at Bert the whole time she talked, waiting for a reaction, but he still didn't look up. "Bert kissed me good-bye, and I went out on the porch to wave to him and Zach as they pulled out. Then when they got back I helped them carry it in. And then Bert gave me a back rub before we went to bed. That was back when he still loved me, though."

I glanced at Bert. He didn't respond.

"What?" I said. "When he still —"

Crystal burst into tears and ran out of the room.

Bert finally looked up, blinking slowly, with a bewildered expression. "Where did she go?" he asked.

"Seriously?" I said. "Did you just miss all that?"

"Our stocks are trending down," he said, frowning at the paper again. "I'd better go take care of it." He got up and wandered blankly out of the kitchen.

So . . . *that* was weird.

I saw Olympia in the den as I was heading up the stairs to shower. "Hey," I said, leaning over the banister. "Can I ask you something?"

"Certainly, dear," she said, putting down her book.

"Where were you and Wilhelm last Tuesday night? While I was out walking around, I mean?"

"Let me see," Olympia said, tapping her chin. "I did some work on our finances, and then we watched a movie, and then he turned into a bat and flew around the yard catching insects for a while, and then we had dinner, and then you came home and I drove you to school. I think that's it."

"Where was Crystal?" I asked.

"She went for a bike ride," Olympia said thoughtfully, "and then I think she lay out on the back roof for a while, getting some moonlight. Oh, and I'm pretty sure she did some online shopping. Packages keep arriving full of clothes that *I* certainly would never order."

"Oh, yeah," I said. "That Crystal. With all the shopping. Hoo, boy." No need to admit that most of that was mine. I didn't want to add *compulsive shopper* next to *murderer* on Olympia's list of my crimes and misdemeanors.

I couldn't tell if Olympia was lying about any of that. In my house everyone minds their own business, for the most part. It would be fairly easy to sneak off, throw a football player out a window, drink his blood, and sneak home again, all without anyone noticing you were gone. Wilhelm could have done it while Olympia thought he was flapping around in bat form. Crystal could have done it while she was out on her bike ride. It could have been any of them.

Zach appeared from his room as I got to the top of the stairs.

"You look terrible," he said, raising his eyebrows.

"Good morning to you, too," I said. "Hey, Zach, where did you and Bert go to get the blood last week?"

"Lexington," he said. "Man, it was really far."

So, no differing stories there. Very unhelpful. "You didn't, like, get back early and just drive

257

d town for a while or anything, huh?"

Zach looked at me funny. "What are you talking about?"

"Nothing," I said, rubbing my face. "I'm going to shower."

I did not want to go to school. I did not want to face Milo or Rowan, and I didn't want to think about math, and I certainly did not want to take a history test. But I had to do all of that because even though I'm a vampire, I still have to graduate from high school. Which I think is wicked lame, but do I have a choice? No.

This was not a day for hot miniskirts. It was a day for my most comfortable jeans and a long-sleeved hunter green top with a black T-shirt on top of it, plus a dark green hoodie. I put the hood up and rested my head on the kitchen island while everyone else finished their mega-gross break-fasts (which for most of them is really dinner, before they head off to sleep away the day).

Zach did that horrible lip-smacking thing he does whenever he finishes one of his "energy shakes." "What's the matter with you?" he said, lifting my hood and peering at me. "Solve Tex's murder yet?"

Olympia turned around from the stove to watch me with her big, dark eyes. I shrugged. "I'm working on it."

"Don't you have to solve it by tomorrow?" Zach said, enjoying himself immensely. "Or else admit you did it, right? Hey, Olympia, you got that padded coffin ready?"

"Did you see Tex last Tuesday?" I asked Zach, resting my head on my arm.

"Yeah, in school," Zach said with a shrug. "We walked out together. Remember, Olympia, you saw him when you picked me up. He came over and said hi."

"Was that him?" Olympia said. "All teenage boys look alike to me. Come on, it's time to go."

I picked up my book bag and followed her out to the car. Cars had mirrors. What if I was all wrong about the locker-room-mirror theory? What if Tex had noticed that Olympia had no reflection in one of the rearview mirrors? Would she have taken drastic measures to protect us? I didn't think she was like that . . . but how well did I know her, after all?

The one piece of good news about the day was that Rowan wasn't at school. I couldn't

here he was, because he had no
ost people probably didn't even notice
e wasn't there. But he'd had a tough night,
too—with any luck, he wouldn't be coming back
to school for a long time.

Milo, on the other hand, was waiting for
me on the front steps. I ducked out of sight and
went in through a side entrance instead. What
could I say to him? *It's not you, it's your life mission
to kill my kind? I'm just not that into your trunk full
of stakes?*

I hid in the library during lunch, but I still
had to go to Art class, and there was no avoiding him there. He jumped up when he saw me.
The expression on his face made me want to cry.
He looked so happy to see me.

I slid reluctantly onto the stool beside him.

"Hey," he said, sitting down again. "How are
you? Are you okay? I tried to call you last night,
but your mom said you were still out—in the
storm and everything—I was worried."

"I'm okay," I said, pulling out my sketch pad.
"I just needed to think."

"About me?" he said anxiously. "Did I do
something wrong?"

260

"It's been a weird week," I said. Yeah. Wild understatement. "You know, starting with the murder and all . . . I guess I was sort of spooked by the whole 'vampire hunter' thing." I dropped my voice to a whisper at the end. And "spooked" didn't actually begin to cover it.

Milo rubbed his temples, looking heart-sick. "I shouldn't have told you. I should have waited."

"No, I'm glad you did," I said. Really, *really* glad, considering I had been about to show him my fangs and all. "You kind of had to. Don't feel bad. But Milo—"

"Oh, no," he said.

"Well, remember I was going to talk to you about something, too?" I had to do this. Hard and fast, like ripping off a Band-Aid.

He nodded. I took a deep breath.

"There's someone else," I said.

Milo looked stricken. "There is? But I thought we—"

"I know," I said. "I'm sorry. I really like you. But I have a boyfriend now, and I wanted to be honest with you. It just worked out that way." I didn't think Daniel would mind this

...on of him, not that he'd be getting ...scription of this conversation or any-... I turned back to my sketch pad and drew for a moment while Milo sat there in stunned silence. I wanted to be nicer. I wanted to give him a hug and tell him how much I wanted to be with him, but obviously I couldn't do any of that.

I looked at him sideways. "I am really sorry."

"No, that's—that's okay," he said in a subdued voice. "We can still be friends, right?"

I smiled awkwardly. "I hope so." *This feeling can't be my heart breaking . . . vampire hearts don't even beat, so how could they break?*

It was the biggest relief when the end of the day finally came, and I managed to get away and walk home by myself without any boys at all.

I wandered through the cemetery for a while, trying to organize my thoughts. I needed new clue sheets. Ones that said *Wilhelm*, *Olympia*, and *Crystal*. And maybe *Bert* and *Zach*, too, although there was no doubt they'd gone out and come back with blood, so I didn't know how else to explain that. Really, I didn't know how to explain any of this.

In the end I went home to drop some more casual, inquisitive questions on them. When I came in, Zach was, as usual, in the process of eating just about everything in our kitchen. He had made himself a giant bowl of nachos, mixing blood in with the salsa.

"Oh, my God, Zach, gross," I said, covering my eyes. "I'm never going to be able to eat salsa again."

"Yum, yum, yum," Zach said, smacking his lips. "You're missing out."

I could not believe I'd ever found this person attractive. To avoid looking at him, I picked up a sheet of paper that was lying next to his books on the table. There was a giant red A+ at the top of the page.

"Whoa," I said. "Is this your calculus exam?"

"Yup," he said smugly.

"Nice work," I said with genuine admiration. "How did you—"

"That's it!" Crystal yelled. She stormed into the kitchen from the den, then turned around to yell back into it. "I don't know what you've done with my husband, *Bert*, but until I get him back, you are sleeping *downstairs* in the *basement*, and I don't *care* if you get *eaten by termites* while you're down there!" She marched right past us and down the hall into her room, slamming the door behind her.

I raised my eyebrows at Zach. "What the heck is going on with them?"

Zach shrugged. "No idea." He stuffed another nacho into his mouth.

I gave him a disgusted look and went into the den, where Bert was sitting at his desk, typing numbers into his calculator as if nothing had just happened.

"Bert?" I said. "Um. Dude?"

He looked over the top of his glasses at me. "Yes, Kira?"

"Is everything okay? Why is Crystal so upset?" I sat down on the couch and folded my legs underneath me.

Bert glanced around with a puzzled look. "Is she?" His gaze drifted back to the pile of papers in front of him. "Oh, dear, this doesn't look right," he muttered, scribbling something in one of the margins.

Now, I'd only lived with Bert and Crystal for a year and a half, but even I knew that this was really bizarre Bert behavior. He cared about Crystal more than anything in the world. He would drop everything for her, even if it meant losing a couple million dollars on a business deal. His whole unlife was about being devoted to her. There was no way normal Bert would ignore her and hurt her feelings the way he'd been doing for the last few days.

Maybe this abnormal Bert was also the kind of guy who killed teenage football stars.

I shoved my hair back, rested my head on the back of the couch, and stared at him while he wrote. He seemed unfazed by my scrutiny.

"Hey, Bert," I said, remembering his strange absences lately, "where were you on Sunday?"

"Sunday," he said blankly.

"During the day," I said. "Zach and I were up around noon, and Crystal came out looking for you, but she couldn't find you."

"Oh," he said. "I was watching TV."

I stared at him. "No, you weren't." Of all the lies to tell, this one was pretty obvious and

265

poorly thought out.

"Yes, I was," he said, in a blunt, sort of mechanical voice. "I watched TV all day. I was right downstairs. Watching TV. All day."

I heard the back door close quietly.

Something clicked in my brain.

I knew who it was. I knew who had murdered Tex.

Chapter 23

A cold wind blew dead leaves in my face as I walked down the street, my boots clopping loudly in the gathering dark.

It didn't matter. I didn't need to be sneaky.

This vampire knew I was coming.

I stepped onto the basketball court behind Luna High School. Tall oak trees towered overhead, and the smooth green grass of the small cemetery stretched off to one side. A discarded basketball sat in the middle of the court, rocking gently.

"I know you're here," I said, stopping at the edge of the white lines. "And I know that you're the one who killed Tex."

There was a rustle in the trees overhead. I looked up as Zach swung off a branch and landed lightly on the ground.

He shoved his hands in his jeans pockets and smirked at me.

"Oh, really, Miss Clever Pants," he said.

"You screwed up," I said. "You got greedy. That's how I figured it out."

Zach rocked back on his heels and tossed his shiny blond hair. "Figured what out?"

"You can mesmerize," I said. "It's like how Wilhelm could turn into a bat right away when he was turned. You had the power as soon as you became a vampire. You mesmerized Bert." He opened his mouth to speak, but I hurried on. "That's how you got your alibi. You mesmerized him to say you went on the blood run, while really you were here, luring Tex to his death."

"An interesting theory," Zach said noncommittally.

"I wouldn't have figured it out, but then you also mesmerized poor Bert to do your calculus exam for you," I said, crossing my arms, "which is, by the way, the most supremely ironic illustration of your laziness and stupidity that I can imagine."

Now Zach was scowling. "I don't call an

A+ stupid," he snapped.

"Oh, and I forgot to add, your selfishness," I said. "Don't you even care that you're messing with Bert's head? Haven't you noticed how weird he's been acting this week? And how it's upsetting Crystal? What if you broke Bert's brain?"

"He'll be fine," Zach scoffed. A slow, sly smile spread across his face. "He's always recovered before."

Cold chills prickled across my skin. "You've done this to him before."

"How else was I supposed to practice?" Zach said with a shrug. "Once I realized I could do it—and with him it's so easy. He's such a malleable guy." He frowned again, taking a step closer to me. "Not like you. You have to be so difficult. You couldn't make things easy for me."

"You tried to mesmerize *me*?" I said indignantly. I remembered the googly eyes he'd been giving me for months. "Oh, my God—is that what all the creepy staring was about?"

His lip curled into a snarl. "My powers are getting stronger all the time. One day I'll succeed, and then we'll be together again, for-ever and always."

"Okay, ew," I said, taking a step back. "But what I don't get is, if you're such a great mes-merizer, why didn't you just convince Tex that he was wrong and you weren't a vampire?"

To my surprise, Zach chuckled. "Oh, you know about that," he said. "You have been busy." He picked up the basketball and began to bounce it slowly from one hand to the other. "Tex was an idiot," he said.

"It sounds like *you* were the idiot," I said. "Letting him see you in the mirror and all. Hello, Vampire 101."

"Yeah, that totally freaked him out," Zach said with a nasty laugh. "He ran away like a startled chicken. But then the dumbass came back when I called him."

"From the school pay phone," I said.

"I told him to meet me here at midnight." Zach shrugged again. "I wasn't planning to kill him."

"Sure," I said. "That's why you set up a whole alibi with Bert."

"Better safe than sorry." Zach dribbled the

basketball behind his back. The long shadows of the oak trees hid his face. Stars were starting to appear in the dark purple sky. "I had Bert drop me off here. And then Tex came, and I showed him what it meant—to be super-strong, to run like the wind, to live forever. I mean, being a vampire is awesome." He spread his hands like this was obvious. I realized he really meant it. Zach loved being a vampire. To him, it didn't suck at all.

"But Tex didn't get it," Zach said, shaking his head. "He was like, 'What about my football scholarship? What about Notre Dame?' Like that matters! Who would pick going to college over *living forever*?"

Um . . . me, I thought.

"So we fought." Zach spun the basketball on his finger. "What can I say? He pissed me off. My original plan was to bite him and *then* kill him—how cool would it be to have a guy my age around the house, right? I mean, Wilhelm and Bert are never going to watch football with me, or help me steal a keg, or crash a beach party. You know? I thought Tex would be cool about it. But he wasn't, and then I figured, well, Plan

B." He stopped the basketball abruptly between his hands. "Kill him and then drink his blood. Turns out it tastes pretty good that way, too." I could see his teeth glinting in the dim light.

"But you were interrupted," I said. "Right?"

"I heard someone coming," Zach said with a nod. "So I ran home, climbed a tree, and waited for Bert to arrive so I could walk in with him. The tree outside your bedroom, I might add." I could *hear* him leering.

"Ew, Zach, can't you stop being gross for one minute?" I said. "Malevolent and lecherous at the same time is kind of overkill."

He took another step toward me. "Overkill," he said softly. "A funny choice of words."

"You're going to confess," I said, trying to sound firm. I didn't like being unable to see his face. "You're going to come home with me and tell Olympia and Wilhelm what happened. They can decide what to do." Hey, this strategy had worked with Rowan. Maybe I had a knack for getting cold-blooded killers to confess to their crimes.

Apparently not. "Oh, I don't think so," Zach said. "I think you have two choices. One, you keep quiet and take whatever punishment our dear vampire parents decide to give you. Personally, I think a stint in a padded coffin would be good for your perspective."

"I'm not the one who needs locking up," I said.

"Or two," Zach went on as if I hadn't spoken, "I kill you right now."

"Oh, please," I said. "I'd like to see you try."

"I wouldn't," said a new voice. "I've got a better idea."

Zach and I turned around. Someone was standing in the shadows under the basketball hoop. He was pointing a crossbow at Zach.

"Option three," said the newcomer. "I kill *you* instead."

Chapter 24

For a heart-stopping moment, I thought it was Milo. I thought he'd finally connected the dots and now he was here to kill me and Zach. I actually thought, *Well, at least this death will be faster than last time.* Then the streetlight beside the basketball court suddenly turned on. Bright yellow light flooded the area, illuminating the court and Zach's furious face and the guy calmly aiming his crossbow at my sort-of-brother's heart.

It wasn't Milo. It was Daniel. I guess that shouldn't have surprised me. He did have a habit of turning up at key moments. Most likely he had been following me since school ended, even though I'd told him to let me handle this.

Besides, Milo was adorable, but he didn't seem like a particularly *successful* vampire hunter, at least from what I'd seen. Oh, I wasn't *un*happy to see Daniel. I wasn't psyched about the pointy wooden thing, but I still liked the fierce hotness of the guy holding it. He didn't look at all bothered by Zach's bulging neck muscles.

"Wait," I said. "Daniel, wait. Don't shoot him."

"Zero tolerance, Kira," Daniel said. "That's our policy. He's tasted human blood; he's dangerous now. We can't have him running around risking all our lives." His eyes shifted to me for a moment. "Especially yours."

"But it's my fault," I said. "I'm the one who turned him. I don't want him to die twice in one year because of me." I stepped in between them and Daniel lowered the crossbow a little, although he didn't put it down. "We can handle this. My parents didn't get rid of me last year when I bit him—they'll know how to deal with Zach."

"I don't need *dealing with*," Zach growled. "I was behaving like a normal vampire should."

"You see?" Daniel said. "It's different with him, Kira. He can't be trusted."

Suddenly Zach grabbed my shoulders and

threw me aside. I crashed into the court's high fence and thudded to the ground. A jolt of pain shot up my wrist and radiated through my whole body.

Zach hurled himself at Daniel, who didn't have time to raise the crossbow. Zach knocked the weapon out of his hands and slammed his fist into Daniel's face. Into Daniel's perfect face! I let out a shout of anger.

"Zach, stop it!" I yelled.

Daniel staggered back but managed to dodge Zach's next punch. He ducked and spun around, kicking Zach hard in the stomach. Zach tumbled, rolled, grabbed Daniel's foot, and yanked him off balance. They rolled across the court, wrestling and punching and, although I'm sure they wouldn't want me to share this, biting and hair pulling as well.

I used the fence to pull myself upright. I was pretty sure Zach had broken my wrist, which was a giant pain because we can't exactly go to hospitals. Olympia would have to fix it, and even though we heal fast, it was still going to hurt *a lot* for a few days.

"Stop!" I shouted again. "Zach, it's over! Leave him alone!"

Of course they didn't listen to me. I spotted the crossbow and ran over to it, but I couldn't figure out how to shoot it. I was pretty sure I'd impale my foot if I tried. But I could still point it.

"Zach, stop it now!" I commanded, aiming the bow at him.

Still not listening. Together they rolled and flailed so fast that I couldn't possibly have hit the right one even if I'd known how to use the stupid thing. Frustrated, I walked over to them, waited until they rolled toward me, and then kicked Zach as hard as I could in the back of the head.

"OW!" he yelled, losing his grip on Daniel. Immediately Daniel seized his hands and wrenched them behind his back. Zach ended up with his face planted into the court. He bellowed something muffled into the pavement, but I think perhaps it was best that we couldn't understand it.

"Kira, give me the crossbow," Daniel said,

kneeling on Zach to hold him down.

"No, this isn't fair," I said. "I mean, I don't like the guy, believe me. But I got a second chance. Shouldn't he get one, too?"

Daniel's gaze shifted over my shoulder. "What do you think?"

I turned around to find Olympia coming through the gate. She glanced up, and I realized Wilhelm must have been looking for us in bat form. A small, dark shape fluttered down from the sky, and a moment later the bat went *poof* and turned into Wilhelm. He looked all craggy and confused about being outside so soon after sunset. His gray hair stuck out in all directions.

"Teenagers," he huffed at Olympia. "I warned you. They're unstable. Too much TV, that's what I say."

Oh, please. He should talk.

"In *my* day—" he started.

"Yes, dear," Olympia interjected. "But they can also learn. I agree with Kira." She gave Daniel a stern, clear-eyed look. "We'll handle it ourselves."

"I'll have to tell my family about this," Daniel said. "I don't know if they'll agree."

Wilhelm snorted. "Wait till they see where we're going to put him," he growled. "He'll be a fine, upstanding member of society by the time he gets out."

Olympia seized the back of Zach's neck, her long fingernails digging into his skin. He let out a yelp. Daniel stood back, and Olympia lifted Zach to his feet.

"Be thankful," she said to him. "A padded coffin is better than you deserve." She marched him off the court, and as they disappeared around the corner of the school I could hear her lecturing him about mesmerizing family members and damaging school property and oh, yeah, murdering people.

Wilhelm grumbled something about pitchforks and stalked off after them, leaving me and Daniel alone on the basketball court.

"Thanks," I said to him. "I mean, not that I needed rescuing or anything, but good effort."

He smiled. "Well, thank *you* for solving the mystery. Not that I wouldn't have figured it out myself eventually, but it was helpful."

I wrinkled my nose at him. "So none of your family members want to stake me anymore, right?"

"I'll tell them everything," Daniel said, pulling me close and putting his arm around me. "They'll be fine. I'm not so sure your family feels very friendly toward me, though."

"Nonsense," I said. "They'll be thrilled that I finally found a nice vampire boy to keep me safe from temptation."

His smile was sweet and wicked at the same time. "Well," he said, "hopefully not *all* temptation."

I lifted my face and our lips met. He tasted like moonlight and mint juleps and the promise that we were going to live forever.

Maybe there were some things about being a vampire that didn't suck at all.